Colonel Chabet

Honoré de Balzac

Pharos Books

ISBN: 978-93-59839-89-9
eISBN: 978-93-59839-43-1

©Publisher

Publisher: Pharos Books (P) Ltd.
Plot No.-63, 1st Floor, Main Mother Dairy Road
Pandav Nagar, East Delhi-110092
Phone: 011-40395855, +4049916623
WhatsApp: +91 9319228272
E-mail: sales@pharosbooks.in
Website: www.pharosbooks.in
First Edition: 2024

Printed By: Sushma Book Binding House, Okhla
Industrial Area, Phase II, New Delhi-110020

COLONEL CHABERT
Honoré de Balzac

DEDICATION

To Madame la Comtesse Ida de Bocarme nee du Chasteler.

COLONEL CHABERT

"HULLO! There is that old Box-coat again!"

This exclamation was made by a lawyer's clerk of the class called in French offices a gutter-jumper—a messenger in fact—who at this moment was eating a piece of dry bread with a hearty appetite. He pulled off a morsel of crumb to make into a bullet, and fired it gleefully through the open pane of the window against which he was leaning. The pellet, well aimed, rebounded almost as high as the window, after hitting the hat of a stranger who was crossing the courtyard of a house in the Rue Vivienne, where dwelt Maitre Derville, attorney-at-law.

"Come, Simonnin, don't play tricks on people, or I will turn you out of doors. However poor a client may be, he is still a man, hang it all!" said the head clerk, pausing in the addition of a bill of costs.

The lawyer's messenger is commonly, as was Simonnin, a lad of thirteen or fourteen, who, in every office, is under the special jurisdiction of the managing clerk, whose errands and *billets-doux* keep him employed on his way to carry writs to the bailiffs and petitions to the Courts. He is akin to the street boy in his habits, and to the pettifogger by fate. The boy is almost always ruthless, unbroken, unmanageable, a ribald rhymester, impudent, greedy, and idle. And yet, almost all these clerklings have an old mother lodging on some fifth floor with whom they share their pittance of thirty or forty francs a month.

"If he is a man, why do you call him old Box-coat?" asked Simonnin, with the air of a schoolboy who has caught out his master.

And he went on eating his bread and cheese, leaning his shoulder against the window jamb; for he rested standing like a cab-horse, one of his legs raised and propped against the other, on the toe of his shoe.

"What trick can we play that cove?" said the third clerk, whose name was Godeschal, in a low voice, pausing in the middle of a discourse he was extemporizing in an appeal engrossed by the fourth clerk, of which copies were being made by two neophytes from the provinces.

Then he went on improvising:

"But, in his noble and beneficent wisdom, his Majesty, Louis the Eighteenth—*(write it at full length, heh! Desroches the learned—you, as you engross it!)*—when he resumed the reins of Government, understood—*(what did that old nincompoop ever understand?)*—the high mission to which he had been called by Divine Providence!—*(a note of admiration and six stops. They are pious enough at the Courts to let us put six)*—and his first thought, as is proved by the date of the order hereinafter designated, was to repair the misfortunes caused by the terrible and sad disasters of the revolutionary times, by restoring to his numerous and faithful adherents—*('numerous' is flattering, and ought to please the Bench)*—all their unsold estates, whether within our realm, or in conquered or acquired territory, or in the endowments of public institutions, for we are, and proclaim ourselves competent to declare, that this is the spirit and meaning of the famous, truly loyal order given in—*Stop," said Godeschal to the three copying clerks, "that rascally sentence brings me to the end of my page.—Well," he went on, wetting the back fold of the sheet with his tongue, so as to be able to fold back the page of thick stamped paper, "well, if you want to play him a trick, tell him that the master can only see his clients between two and three in the morning; we shall see if he comes, the old ruffian!"*

And Godeschal took up the sentence he was dictating—*"given in—*Are you ready?"

"Yes," cried the three writers.

It all went all together, the appeal, the gossip, and the conspiracy.

"*Given in*—Here, Daddy Boucard, what is the date of the order? We must dot our *i*'s and cross our *t*'s, by Jingo! it helps to fill the pages."

"By Jingo!" repeated one of the copying clerks before Boucard, the head clerk, could reply.

"What! have you written *by Jingo?*" cried Godeschal, looking at one of the novices, with an expression at once stern and humorous.

"Why, yes," said Desroches, the fourth clerk, leaning across his neighbor's copy, "he has written, '*We must dot our i's*' and spelt it *by Gingo!*"

All the clerks shouted with laughter.

"Why! Monsieur Hure, you take 'By Jingo' for a law term, and you say you come from Mortagne!" exclaimed Simonnin.

"Scratch it cleanly out," said the head clerk. "If the judge, whose business it is to tax the bill, were to see such things, he would say you were laughing at the whole boiling. You would hear of it from the chief! Come, no more of this nonsense, Monsieur Hure! A Norman ought not to write out an appeal without thought. It is the 'Shoulder arms!' of the law."

"*Given in—in?*" asked Godeschal.—"Tell me when, Boucard."

"June 1814," replied the head clerk, without looking up from his work.

A knock at the office door interrupted the circumlocutions of the prolix document. Five clerks with rows of hungry teeth, bright, mocking eyes, and curly heads, lifted their noses towards the door, after crying all together in a singing tone, "Come in!"

Boucard kept his face buried in a pile of papers—*broutilles* (odds and ends) in French law jargon—and went on drawing out the bill of costs on which he was busy.

The office was a large room furnished with the traditional stool which is to be seen in all these dens of law-quibbling. The stovepipe crossed the room diagonally to the chimney of a bricked-up fireplace; on the marble chimney-piece were several chunks of bread, triangles of Brie cheese, pork cutlets, glasses, bottles, and the head clerk's cup of chocolate. The smell of these dainties blended so completely with that of the immoderately overheated stove and the odor peculiar to offices and old papers, that the trail of a fox would not have been perceptible. The floor was covered with mud and snow, brought in by the clerks. Near the window stood the desk with a revolving lid, where the head clerk worked, and against the back of it was the second clerk's table. The second clerk was at this moment in Court. It was between eight and nine in the morning.

The only decoration of the office consisted in huge yellow posters, announcing seizures of real estate, sales, settlements under trust, final or interim judgments,—all the glory of a lawyer's office. Behind the head clerk was an enormous room, of which each division was crammed with bundles of papers with an infinite number of tickets hanging from them at the ends of red tape, which give a peculiar physiognomy to law papers. The lower rows were filled with cardboard boxes, yellow with use, on which might be read the names of the more important clients whose cases were juicily stewing at this present time. The dirty window-panes admitted but little daylight. Indeed, there are very few offices in Paris where it is possible to write without lamplight before ten in the morning in the month of February, for they are all left to very natural neglect; every one comes and no one stays; no one has any personal interest in a scene of mere routine— neither the attorney, nor the counsel, nor the clerks, trouble themselves about the appearance of a place which, to the youths, is a schoolroom; to the clients, a passage; to the chief, a laboratory. The greasy furniture is handed down to successive owners with such scrupulous care, that in some offices may still be seen boxes of *remainders*, machines for twisting parchment gut, and bags left by the prosecuting parties of the Chatelet (abbreviated to *Chlet*)—a Court which, under the old order of things, represented the present Court of First Instance (or County Court).

So in this dark office, thick with dust, there was, as in all its fellows, something repulsive to the clients—something which made it one of the most hideous monstrosities of Paris. Nay, were it not for the mouldy sacristies where prayers are weighed out and paid for like groceries, and for the old-clothes shops, where flutter the rags that blight all the illusions of life by showing us the last end of all our festivities—an attorney's office would be, of all social marts, the most loathsome. But we might say the same of the gambling-hell, of the Law Court, of the lottery office, of the brothel.

But why? In these places, perhaps, the drama being played in a man's soul makes him indifferent to accessories, which would also account for the single-mindedness of great thinkers and men of great ambitions.

"Where is my penknife?"

"I am eating my breakfast."

"You go and be hanged! here is a blot on the copy."

"Silence, gentlemen!"

These various exclamations were uttered simultaneously at the moment when the old client shut the door with the sort of humility which disfigures the movements of a man down on his luck. The stranger tried to smile, but the muscles of his face relaxed as he vainly looked for some symptoms of amenity on the inexorably indifferent faces of the six clerks. Accustomed, no doubt, to gauge men, he very politely addressed the gutter-jumper, hoping to get a civil answer from this boy of all work.

"Monsieur, is your master at home?"

The pert messenger made no reply, but patted his ear with the fingers of his left hand, as much as to say, "I am deaf."

"What do you want, sir?" asked Godeschal, swallowing as he spoke a mouthful of bread big enough to charge a four-pounder, flourishing his knife and crossing his legs, throwing up one foot in the air to the level of his eyes.

"This is the fifth time I have called," replied the victim. "I wish to speak to M. Derville."

"On business?"

"Yes, but I can explain it to no one but—"

"M. Derville is in bed; if you wish to consult him on some difficulty, he does no serious work till midnight. But if you will lay the case before us, we could help you just as well as he can to——"

The stranger was unmoved; he looked timidly about him, like a dog who has got into a strange kitchen and expects a kick. By grace of their profession, lawyers' clerks have no fear of thieves; they did not suspect the owner of the box-coat, and left him to study the place, where he looked in vain for a chair to sit on, for he was evidently tired. Attorneys, on principle, do not have many chairs in their offices. The inferior client, being kept waiting on his feet, goes away grumbling, but then he does not waste time, which, as an old lawyer once said, is not allowed for when the bill is taxed.

"Monsieur," said the old man, "as I have already told you, I cannot explain my business to any one but M. Derville. I will wait till he is up."

Boucard had finished his bill. He smelt the fragrance of his chocolate, rose from his cane armchair, went to the chimney-piece, looked the old man from head to foot, stared at his coat, and made an indescribable grimace. He probably reflected that whichever way his client might be wrung, it would be impossible to squeeze out a centime, so he put in a few brief words to rid the office of a bad customer.

"It is the truth, monsieur. The chief only works at night. If your business is important, I recommend you to return at one in the morning." The stranger looked at the head clerk with a bewildered expression, and remained motionless for a moment. The clerks, accustomed to every change of countenance, and the odd whimsicalities to which indecision or absence of mind gives rise in "parties," went on eating, making as much noise with their jaws as horses over a manger, and paying no further heed to the old man.

"I will come again to-night," said the stranger at length, with the tenacious desire, peculiar to the unfortunate, to catch humanity at fault.

The only irony allowed to poverty is to drive Justice and Benevolence to unjust denials. When a poor wretch has convicted Society of falsehood, he throws himself more eagerly on the mercy of God.

"What do you think of that for a cracked pot?" said Simonnin, without waiting till the old man had shut the door.

"He looks as if he had been buried and dug up again," said a clerk.

"He is some colonel who wants his arrears of pay," said the head clerk.

"No, he is a retired concierge," said Godeschal.

"I bet you he is a nobleman," cried Boucard.

"I bet you he has been a porter," retorted Godeschal. "Only porters are gifted by nature with shabby box-coats, as worn and greasy and frayed as that old body's. And did you see his trodden-down boots that let the water in, and his stock which serves for a shirt? He has slept in a dry arch."

"He may be of noble birth, and yet have pulled the doorlatch," cried Desroches. "It has been known!"

"No," Boucard insisted, in the midst of laughter, "I maintain that he was a brewer in 1789, and a colonel in the time of the Republic."

"I bet theatre tickets round that he never was a soldier," said Godeschal.

"Done with you," answered Boucard.

"Monsieur! Monsieur!" shouted the little messenger, opening the window.

"What are you at now, Simonnin?" asked Boucard.

"I am calling him that you may ask him whether he is a colonel or a porter; he must know."

All the clerks laughed. As to the old man, he was already coming upstairs again.

"What can we say to him?" cried Godeschal.

"Leave it to me," replied Boucard.

The poor man came in nervously, his eyes cast down, perhaps not to betray how hungry he was by looking too greedily at the eatables.

"Monsieur," said Boucard, "will you have the kindness to leave your name, so that M. Derville may know——"

"Chabert."

"The Colonel who was killed at Eylau?" asked Hure, who, having so far said nothing, was jealous of adding a jest to all the others.

"The same, monsieur," replied the good man, with antique simplicity. And he went away.

"Whew!"

"Done brown!"

"Poof!"

"Oh!"

"Ah!"

"Boum!"

"The old rogue!"

"Ting-a-ring-ting!"

"Sold again!"

"Monsieur Desroches, you are going to the play without paying," said Hure to the fourth clerk, giving him a slap on the shoulder that might have killed a rhinoceros.

There was a storm of cat-calls, cries, and exclamations, which all the onomatopeia of the language would fail to represent.

"Which theatre shall we go to?"

"To the opera," cried the head clerk.

"In the first place," said Godeschal, "I never mentioned which theatre. I might, if I chose, take you to see Madame Saqui."

"Madame Saqui is not the play."

"What is a play?" replied Godeschal. "First, we must define the point of fact. What did I bet, gentlemen? A play. What is a play? A spectacle. What is a spectacle? Something to be seen—"

"But on that principle you would pay your bet by taking us to see the water run under the Pont Neuf!" cried Simonnin, interrupting him.

"To be seen for money," Godeschal added.

"But a great many things are to be seen for money that are not plays. The definition is defective," said Desroches.

"But do listen to me!"

"You are talking nonsense, my dear boy," said Boucard.

"Is Curtius' a play?" said Godeschal.

"No," said the head clerk, "it is a collection of figures—but it is a spectacle."

"I bet you a hundred francs to a sou," Godeschal resumed, "that Curtius' Waxworks forms such a show as might be called a play or theatre. It contains a thing to be seen at various prices, according to the place you choose to occupy."

"And so on, and so forth!" said Simonnin.

"You mind I don't box your ears!" said Godeschal.

The clerk shrugged their shoulders.

"Besides, it is not proved that that old ape was not making game of us," he said, dropping his argument, which was drowned in the laughter of the other clerks. "On my honor, Colonel Chabert is really and truly dead. His wife is married again to Comte Ferraud, Councillor of State. Madame Ferraud is one of our clients."

"Come, the case is remanded till to-morrow," said Boucard. "To work, gentlemen. The deuce is in it; we get nothing done here. Finish copying that appeal; it must be handed in before the sitting of the Fourth Chamber, judgment is to be given to-day. Come, on you go!"

"If he really were Colonel Chabert, would not that impudent rascal Simonnin have felt the leather of his boot in the right place when he pretended to be deaf?" said Desroches, regarding this remark as more conclusive than Godeschal's.

"Since nothing is settled," said Boucard, "let us all agree to go to the upper boxes of the Francais and see Talma in 'Nero.' Simonnin may go to the pit."

And thereupon the head clerk sat down at his table, and the others followed his example.

"Given in June eighteen hundred and fourteen *(in words),*" *said Godeschal. "Ready?"*

"Yes," replied the two copying-clerks and the engrosser, whose pens forthwith began to creak over the stamped paper, making as much noise in the office as a hundred cockchafers imprisoned by schoolboys in paper cages.

"*And we hope that my lords on the Bench,*" the extemporizing clerk went on. "Stop! I must read my sentence through again. I do not understand it myself."

"Forty-six (that must often happen) and three forty-nines," said Boucard.

"We hope," *Godeschal began again, after reading all through the document,* "that my lords on the Bench will not be less magnanimous than the august author of the decree, and that they will do justice against the miserable claims of the acting committee of the chief Board of the Legion of Honor by interpreting the law in the wide sense we have here set forth——"

"Monsieur Godeschal, wouldn't you like a glass of water?" said the little messenger.

"That imp of a boy!" said Boucard. "Here, get on your double-soled shanks-mare, take this packet, and spin off to the Invalides."

"Here set forth," *Godeschal went on.* "*Add* in the interest of Madame la Vicomtesse *(at full length)* de Grandlieu. "

"What!" cried the chief, "are you thinking of drawing up an appeal in the case of Vicomtesse de Grandlieu against the Legion of Honor—a case for the office to stand or fall by? You are something like an ass! Have the goodness to put aside your copies and your notes; you may keep all that for the case of Navarreins against the Hospitals. It is late. I will draw up a little petition myself, with a due allowance of 'inasmuch,' and go to the Courts myself."

This scene is typical of the thousand delights which, when we look back on our youth, make us say, "Those were good times."

At about one in the morning Colonel Chabert, self-styled, knocked at the door of Maitre Derville, attorney to the Court of First Instance in the Department of the Seine. The porter told him that Monsieur Derville had not yet come in. The old man said he had an appointment, and was shown upstairs to the rooms occupied by the famous lawyer, who, notwithstanding his youth, was considered to have one of the longest heads in Paris.

Having rung, the distrustful applicant was not a little astonished at finding the head clerk busily arranging in a convenient order on his master's dining-room table the papers relating to the cases to be tried on the morrow. The clerk, not less astonished, bowed to the Colonel and begged him to take a seat, which the client did.

"On my word, monsieur, I thought you were joking yesterday when you named such an hour for an interview," said the old man, with the forced mirth of a ruined man, who does his best to smile.

"The clerks were joking, but they were speaking the truth too," replied the man, going on with his work. "M. Derville chooses this hour for studying his cases, taking stock of their possibilities, arranging how to conduct them, deciding on the line of defence. His prodigious intellect is freer at this hour—the only time when he can have the silence and quiet needed for the conception of good ideas. Since he entered the profession, you are the third person to come to him for a consultation at this midnight hour. After coming in the chief will discuss each case, read everything, spend four or five hours perhaps over the business, then he will ring for me and explain to me his intentions. In the morning from ten to two he hears what his clients have to say, then he spends the rest of his day in appointments. In the evening he goes into society to keep up his connections. So he has only the night for undermining his cases, ransacking the arsenal of the code, and laying his plan of battle. He is determined never to lose a case; he loves his art. He will not undertake every case, as his brethren do. That is his life, an exceptionally active one. And he makes a great deal of money."

As he listened to this explanation, the old man sat silent, and his strange face assumed an expression so bereft of intelligence, that the clerk, after looking at him, thought no more about him.

A few minutes later Derville came in, in evening dress; his head clerk opened the door to him, and went back to finish arranging the papers. The young lawyer paused for a moment in amazement on seeing in the dim light the strange client who awaited him. Colonel Chabert was as absolutely immovable as one of the wax figures in Curtius' collection to which Godeschal had proposed to treat his fellow-clerks. This quiescence would not have been a subject for astonishment if it had not completed the supernatural aspect of the man's whole person. The old soldier was dry and lean. His forehead, intentionally hidden under a smoothly combed wig, gave him a look of mystery. His eyes seemed shrouded in a transparent film; you would have compared them to dingy mother-of-pearl with a blue iridescence changing in the gleam of the wax lights. His face, pale, livid, and as thin as a knife, if I may use such a vulgar expression, was as the face of the dead. Round his neck was a tight black silk stock.

Below the dark line of this rag the body was so completely hidden in shadow that a man of imagination might have supposed the old head was due to some chance play of light and shade, or have taken it for a portrait by Rembrandt, without a frame. The brim of the hat which covered the old man's brow cast a black line of shadow on the upper part of the face. This grotesque effect, though natural, threw into relief by contrast the white furrows, the cold wrinkles, the colorless tone of the corpse-like countenance. And the absence of all movement in the figure, of all fire in the eye, were in harmony with a certain look of melancholy madness, and the deteriorating symptoms characteristic of senility, giving the face an indescribably ill-starred look which no human words could render.

But an observer, especially a lawyer, could also have read in this stricken man the signs of deep sorrow, the traces of grief which had worn into this face, as drops of water from the sky falling on fine marble at last destroy its beauty. A physician, an author, or a judge might have discerned a whole drama at the sight of its sublime horror, while the least charm was its resemblance to the grotesques which artists amuse themselves by sketching on a corner of the lithographic stone while chatting with a friend.

On seeing the attorney, the stranger started, with the convulsive thrill that comes over a poet when a sudden noise rouses him from a fruitful reverie in silence and at night. The old man hastily removed his hat and rose to bow to the young man; the leather lining of his hat was doubtless very greasy; his wig stuck to it without his noticing it, and left his head bare, showing his skull horribly disfigured by a scar beginning at the nape of the neck and ending over the right eye, a prominent seam all across his head. The sudden removal of the dirty wig which the poor man wore to hide this gash gave the two lawyers no inclination to laugh, so horrible to behold was this riven skull. The first idea suggested by the sight of this old wound was, "His intelligence must have escaped through that cut."

"If this is not Colonel Chabert, he is some thorough-going trooper!" thought Boucard.

"Monsieur," said Derville, "to whom have I the honor of speaking?"

"To Colonel Chabert."

"Which?"

"He who was killed at Eylau," replied the old man.

On hearing this strange speech, the lawyer and his clerk glanced at each other, as much as to say, "He is mad."

"Monsieur," the Colonel went on, "I wish to confide to you the secret of my position."

A thing worthy of note is the natural intrepidity of lawyers. Whether from the habit of receiving a great many persons, or from the deep sense of the protection conferred on them by the law, or from confidence in their missions, they enter everywhere, fearing nothing, like priests and physicians. Derville signed to Boucard, who vanished.

"During the day, sir," said the attorney, "I am not so miserly of my time, but at night every minute is precious. So be brief and concise. Go to the facts without digression. I will ask for any explanations I may consider necessary. Speak."

Having bid his strange client to be seated, the young man sat down at the table; but while he gave his attention to the deceased Colonel, he turned over the bundles of papers.

"You know, perhaps," said the dead man, "that I commanded a cavalry regiment at Eylau. I was of important service to the success of Murat's famous charge which decided the victory. Unhappily for me, my death is a historical fact, recorded in *Victoires et Conquetes*, where it is related in full detail. We cut through the three Russian lines, which at once closed up and formed again, so that we had to repeat the movement back again. At the moment when we were nearing the Emperor, after having scattered the Russians, I came against a squadron of the enemy's cavalry. I rushed at the obstinate brutes. Two Russian officers, perfect giants, attacked me both at once. One of them gave me a cut across the head that crashed through everything, even a black silk cap I wore next my head, and cut deep into the skull. I fell from my horse. Murat came up to support me. He rode over my body, he and all his men, fifteen hundred of them—there might have been more! My death was announced to the Emperor, who as a precaution—for he was fond of me, was the master—wished to know if there were no hope of saving the man he had to thank for such a vigorous attack. He sent two surgeons to identify me and bring me into Hospital, saying, perhaps too carelessly, for he was very busy, 'Go and see whether by any chance poor Chabert is still alive.' These rascally saw-bones, who had just seen me lying under the hoofs of the horses of two regiments, no doubt did not trouble themselves to feel my pulse, and reported that I was quite dead. The certificate of death was probably made out in accordance with the rules of military jurisprudence."

As he heard his visitor express himself with complete lucidity, and relate a story so probable though so strange, the young lawyer ceased fingering the papers, rested his left elbow on the table, and with his head on his hand looked steadily at the Colonel.

"Do you know, monsieur, that I am lawyer to the Countess Ferraud," he said, interrupting the speaker, "Colonel Chabert's widow?"

"My wife—yes monsieur. Therefore, after a hundred fruitless attempts to interest lawyers, who have all thought me mad, I made up my mind to come to you. I will tell you of my misfortunes afterwards; for the present, allow me to prove the facts, explaining rather how things must have fallen out rather than how they did occur. Certain circumstances, known, I suppose to no one but the Almighty, compel me to speak of some things as hypothetical. The wounds I had received must presumably have produced tetanus, or have thrown me into a state analogous to that of a disease called, I believe, catalepsy. Otherwise how is it conceivable that I should have been stripped, as is the custom in time of the war, and thrown into the common grave by the men ordered to bury the dead?

"Allow me here to refer to a detail of which I could know nothing till after the event, which, after all, I must speak of as my death. At Stuttgart, in 1814, I met an old quartermaster of my regiment. This dear fellow, the only man who chose to recognize me, and of whom I will tell you more later, explained the marvel of my preservation, by telling me that my horse was shot in the flank at the moment when I was wounded. Man and beast went down together, like a monk cut out of card-paper. As I fell, to the right or to the left, I was no doubt covered by the body of my horse, which protected me from being trampled to death or hit by a ball.

"When I came to myself, monsieur, I was in a position and an atmosphere of which I could give you no idea if I talked till to-morrow. The little air there was to breathe was foul. I wanted to move, and found no room. I opened my eyes, and saw nothing. The most alarming circumstance was the lack of air, and this enlightened me as to my situation. I understood that no fresh air could penetrate to me, and that I must die. This thought took off the sense of intolerable pain which had aroused me. There was a violent singing in my ears. I heard—or I thought I heard, I will assert nothing—groans from the world of dead among whom I was lying. Some nights I still think I hear those stifled moans; though the remembrance of that time is very obscure, and my memory very indistinct, in spite of my impressions of far more acute suffering I was fated to go through, and which have confused my ideas.

"But there was something more awful than cries; there was a silence such as I have never known elsewhere—literally, the silence of the grave. At last, by raising my hands and feeling the dead, I discerned a vacant space between my head and the human carrion above. I could thus measure the space, granted by a chance of which I knew not the cause. It would seem that, thanks to the carelessness and the haste with which we had been pitched into the trench, two dead bodies had leaned across and against each other, forming an angle like that made by two cards when a child is building a card castle. Feeling about me at once, for there was no time for play, I happily felt an arm lying detached, the arm of a Hercules! A stout bone, to which I owed my rescue. But for this unhoped-for help, I must have perished. But with a fury you may imagine, I began to work my way through the bodies which separated me from the layer of earth which had no doubt been thrown over us—I say us, as if there had been others living! I worked with a will, monsieur, for here I am! But to this day I do not know how I succeeded in getting through the pile of flesh which formed a barrier between me and life. You will say I had three arms. This crowbar, which I used cleverly enough, opened out a little air between the bodies I moved, and I economized my breath. At last I saw daylight, but through snow!

"At that moment I perceived that my head was cut open. Happily my blood, or that of my comrades, or perhaps the torn skin of my horse, who knows, had in coagulating formed a sort of natural plaster. But, in spite of it, I fainted away when my head came into contact with the snow. However, the little warmth left in me melted the snow about me; and when I recovered consciousness, I found myself in the middle of a round hole, where I stood shouting as long as I could. But the sun was rising, so I had very little chance of being heard. Was there any one in the fields yet? I pulled myself up, using my feet as a spring, resting on one of the dead, whose ribs were firm. You may suppose that this was not the moment for saying, 'Respect courage in misfortune!' In short, monsieur, after enduring the anguish, if the word is strong enough for my frenzy, of seeing for a long time, yes, quite a long time, those cursed Germans flying from a voice they heard where they could see no one, I was dug out by a woman, who was brave or curious enough to come close to my head, which must have looked as though it had sprouted from the ground like a mushroom. This woman went to fetch her husband, and between them they got me to their poor hovel.

"It would seem that I must have again fallen into a catalepsy—allow me to use the word to describe a state of which I have no idea, but which, from the account given by my hosts, I suppose to have been the effect of that malady. I remained for six months between life and death; not speaking, or, if I spoke, talking in delirium. At last, my hosts got me admitted to the hospital at Heilsberg.

"You will understand, Monsieur, that I came out of the womb of the grave as naked as I came from my mother's; so that six months afterwards, when I remembered, one fine morning, that I had been Colonel Chabert, and when, on recovering my wits, I tried to exact from my nurse rather more respect than she paid to any poor devil, all my companions in the ward began to laugh. Luckily for me, the surgeon, out of professional pride, had answered for my cure, and was naturally interested in his patient. When I told him coherently about my former life, this good man, named Sparchmann, signed a deposition, drawn up in the legal form of his country, giving an account of the miraculous way in which I had escaped from the trench dug for the dead, the day and hour when I had been found by my benefactress and her husband, the nature and exact spot of my injuries, adding to these documents a description of my person.

"Well, monsieur, I have neither these important pieces of evidence, nor the declaration I made before a notary at Heilsberg, with a view to establishing my identity. From the day when I was turned out of that town by the events of the war, I have wandered about like a vagabond, begging my bread, treated as a madman when I have told my story, without ever having found or earned a sou to enable me to recover the deeds which would prove my statements, and restore me to society. My sufferings have often kept me for six months at a time in some little town, where every care was taken of the invalid Frenchman, but where he was laughed at to his face as soon as he said he was Colonel Chabert. For a long time that laughter, those doubts, used to put me into rages which did me harm, and which even led to my being locked up at Stuttgart as a madman. And indeed, as you may judge from my story, there was ample reason for shutting a man up.

"At the end of two years' detention, which I was compelled to submit to, after hearing my keepers say a thousand times, 'Here is a poor man who thinks he is Colonel Chabert' to people who would reply, 'Poor fellow!' I became convinced of the impossibility of my own adventure. I grew melancholy, resigned, and quiet, and gave up calling myself Colonel Chabert, in order to get out of my prison, and see France once more. Oh, monsieur! To see Paris again was a delirium which I—"

Without finishing his sentence, Colonel Chabert fell into a deep study, which Derville respected.

"One fine day," his visitor resumed, "one spring day, they gave me the key of the fields, as we say, and ten thalers, admitting that I talked quite sensibly on all subjects, and no longer called myself Colonel Chabert. On my honor, at that time, and even to this day, sometimes I hate my name. I wish I were not myself. The sense of my rights kills me. If my illness had but deprived me of all memory of my past life, I could be happy. I should have entered the service again under any name, no matter what, and should, perhaps, have been made Field-Marshal in Austria or Russia. Who knows?"

"Monsieur," said the attorney, "you have upset all my ideas. I feel as if I heard you in a dream. Pause for a moment, I beg of you."

"You are the only person," said the Colonel, with a melancholy look, "who ever listened to me so patiently. No lawyer has been willing to lend me ten napoleons to enable me to procure from Germany the necessary documents to begin my lawsuit—"

"What lawsuit?" said the attorney, who had forgotten his client's painful position in listening to the narrative of his past sufferings.

"Why, monsieur, is not the Comtesse Ferraud my wife? She has thirty thousand francs a year, which belong to me, and she will not give me a son. When I tell lawyers these things—men of sense; when I propose—I, a beggar—to bring action against a Count and Countess; when I—a dead man—bring up as against a certificate of death a certificate of marriage and registers of births, they show me out, either with the air of cold politeness, which you all know how to assume to rid yourself of a hapless wretch, or brutally, like men who think they have to deal with a swindler or a madman—it depends on their nature. I have been buried under the dead; but now I am buried under the living, under papers, under facts, under the whole of society, which wants to shove me underground again!"

"Pray resume your narrative," said Derville.

"'Pray resume it!'" cried the hapless old man, taking the young lawyer's hand. "That is the first polite word I have heard since—"

The Colonel wept. Gratitude choked his voice. The appealing and unutterable eloquence that lies in the eyes, in a gesture, even in silence, entirely convinced Derville, and touched him deeply.

"Listen, monsieur," said he; "I have this evening won three hundred francs at cards. I may very well lay out half that sum in making a man happy. I will begin the inquiries and researches necessary to obtain the documents of which you speak, and until they arrive I will give you five francs a day. If you are Colonel Chabert, you will pardon the smallness of the loan as it is coming from a young man who has his fortune to make. Proceed."

The Colonel, as he called himself, sat for a moment motionless and bewildered; the depth of his woes had no doubt destroyed his powers of belief. Though he was eager in pursuit of his military distinction, of his fortune, of himself, perhaps it was in obedience to the inexplicable feeling, the latent germ in every man's heart, to which we owe the experiments of alchemists, the passion for glory, the discoveries of astronomy and of physics, everything which prompts man to expand his being by multiplying himself through deeds or ideas. In his mind the *Ego* was now but a secondary object, just as the vanity of success or the pleasures of winning become dearer to the gambler than the object he has at stake. The young lawyer's words were as a miracle to this man, for ten years repudiated by his wife, by justice, by the whole social creation. To find in a lawyer's office the ten gold pieces which had so long been refused him by so many people, and in so many ways! The colonel was like the lady who, having been ill of a fever for fifteen years, fancied she had some fresh complaint when she was cured. There are joys in which we have ceased to believe; they fall on us, it is like a thunderbolt; they burn us. The poor man's gratitude was too great to find utterance. To superficial observers he seemed cold, but Derville saw complete honesty under this amazement. A swindler would have found his voice.

"Where was I?" said the Colonel, with the simplicity of a child or of a soldier, for there is often something of the child in a true soldier, and almost always something of the soldier in a child, especially in France.

"At Stuttgart. You were out of prison," said Derville.

"You know my wife?" asked the Colonel.

"Yes," said Derville, with a bow.

"What is she like?"

"Still quite charming."

The old man held up his hand, and seemed to be swallowing down some secret anguish with the grave and solemn resignation that is characteristic of men who have stood the ordeal of blood and fire on the battlefield.

"Monsieur," said he, with a sort of cheerfulness—for he breathed again, the poor Colonel; he had again risen from the grave; he had just melted a covering of snow less easily thawed than that which had once before frozen his head; and he drew a deep breath, as if he had just escaped from a dungeon—"Monsieur, if I had been a handsome young fellow, none of my misfortunes would have befallen me. Women believe in men when they flavor their speeches with the word Love. They hurry then, they come, they go, they are everywhere at once; they intrigue, they assert facts, they play the very devil for a man who takes their fancy. But how could I interest a woman? I had a face like a Requiem. I was dressed like a *sans-culotte*. I was more like an Esquimaux than a Frenchman—I, who had formerly been considered one of the smartest of fops in 1799!—I, Chabert, Count of the Empire.

"Well, on the very day when I was turned out into the streets like a dog, I met the quartermaster of whom I just now spoke. This old soldier's name was Boutin. The poor devil and I made the queerest pair of broken-down hacks I ever set eyes on. I met him out walking; but though I recognized him, he could not possibly guess who I was. We went into a tavern together. In there, when I told him my name, Boutin's mouth opened from ear to ear in a roar of laughter, like the bursting of a mortar. That mirth, monsieur, was one of the keenest pangs I have known. It told me without disguise how great were the changes in me! I was, then, unrecognizable even to the humblest and most grateful of my former friends!

"I had once saved Boutin's life, but it was only the repayment of a debt I owed him. I need not tell you how he did me this service; it was at Ravenna, in Italy. The house where Boutin prevented my being stabbed was not extremely respectable. At that time I was not a colonel, but, like Boutin himself, a common trooper. Happily there were certain details of this adventure which could be known only to us two, and when I recalled them to his mind his incredulity diminished. I then told him the story of my singular experiences. Although my eyes and my voice, he told me, were strangely altered, although I had neither hair, teeth, nor eyebrows, and was as colorless as an Albino, he at last recognized his Colonel in the beggar, after a thousand questions, which I answered triumphantly.

"He related his adventures; they were not less extraordinary than my own; he had lately come back from the frontiers of China, which he had tried to cross after escaping from Siberia. He told me of the catastrophe of the Russian campaign, and of Napoleon's first abdication. That news was one of the things which caused me most anguish!

                                        COLONEL CHABERT

"We were two curious derelicts, having been rolled over the globe as pebbles are rolled by the ocean when storms bear them from shore to shore. Between us we had seen Egypt, Syria, Spain, Russia, Holland, Germany, Italy and Dalmatia, England, China, Tartary, Siberia; the only thing wanting was that neither of us had been to America or the Indies. Finally, Boutin, who still was more locomotive than I, undertook to go to Paris as quickly as might be to inform my wife of the predicament in which I was. I wrote a long letter full of details to Madame Chabert. That, monsieur, was the fourth! If I had had any relations, perhaps nothing of all this might have happened; but, to be frank with you, I am but a workhouse child, a soldier, whose sole fortune was his courage, whose sole family is mankind at large, whose country is France, whose only protector is the Almighty.—Nay, I am wrong! I had a father—the Emperor! Ah! if he were but here, the dear man! If he could see *his Chabert*, as he used to call me, in the state in which I am now, he would be in a rage! What is to be done? Our sun is set, and we are all out in the cold now. After all, political events might account for my wife's silence!

"Boutin set out. He was a lucky fellow! He had two bears, admirably trained, which brought him in a living. I could not go with him; the pain I suffered forbade my walking long stages. I wept, monsieur, when we parted, after I had gone as far as my state allowed in company with him and his bears. At Carlsruhe I had an attack of neuralgia in the head, and lay for six weeks on straw in an inn. I should never have ended if I were to tell you all the distresses of my life as a beggar. Moral suffering, before which physical suffering pales, nevertheless excites less pity, because it is not seen. I remember shedding tears, as I stood in front of a fine house in Strassburg where once I had given an entertainment, and where nothing was given me, not even a piece of bread. Having agreed with Boutin on the road I was to take, I went to every post-office to ask if there were a letter or some money for me. I arrived at Paris without having found either. What despair I had been forced to endure! 'Boutin must be dead!

I told myself, and in fact the poor fellow was killed at Waterloo. I heard of his death later, and by mere chance. His errand to my wife had, of course, been fruitless.

"At last I entered Paris—with the Cossacks. To me this was grief on grief. On seeing the Russians in France, I quite forgot that I had no shoes on my feet nor money in my pocket. Yes, monsieur, my clothes were in tatters. The evening before I reached Paris I was obliged to bivouac in the woods of Claye. The chill of the night air no doubt brought on an attack of some nameless complaint which seized me as I was crossing the Faubourg Saint-Martin. I dropped almost senseless at the door of an ironmonger's shop. When I recovered I was in a bed in the Hotel-Dieu. There I stayed very contentedly for about a month. I was then turned out; I had no money, but I was well, and my feet were on the good stones of Paris. With what delight and haste did I make my way to the Rue du Mont-Blanc, where my wife should be living in a house belonging to me! Bah! the Rue du Mont-Blanc was now the Rue de la Chausee d'Antin; I could not find my house; it had been sold and pulled down. Speculators had built several houses over my gardens. Not knowing that my wife had married M. Ferraud, I could obtain no information.

"At last I went to the house of an old lawyer who had been in charge of my affairs. This worthy man was dead, after selling his connection to a younger man. This gentleman informed me, to my great surprise, of the administration of my estate, the settlement of the moneys, of my wife's marriage, and the birth of her two children. When I told him that I was Colonel Chabert, he laughed so heartily that I left him without saying another word. My detention at Stuttgart had suggested possibilities of Charenton, and I determined to act with caution. Then, monsieur, knowing where my wife lived, I went to her house, my heart high with hope.—Well," said the Colonel, with a gesture of concentrated fury, "when I called under an assumed name I was not admitted, and on the day when I used my own I was turned out of doors.

"To see the Countess come home from a ball or the play in the early morning, I have sat whole nights through, crouching close to the wall of her gateway. My eyes pierced the depths of the carriage, which flashed past me with the swiftness of lightning, and I caught a glimpse of the woman who is my wife and no longer mine. Oh, from that day I have lived for vengeance!" cried the old man in a hollow voice, and suddenly standing up in front of Derville. "She knows that I am alive; since my return she has had two letters written with my own hand. She loves me no more!—I—I know not whether I love or hate her. I long for her and curse her by turns. To me she owes all her fortune, all her happiness; well, she has not sent me the very smallest pittance. Sometimes I do not know what will become of me!"

With these words the veteran dropped on to his chair again and remained motionless. Derville sat in silence, studying his client.

"It is a serious business," he said at length, mechanically. "Even granting the genuineness of the documents to be procured from Heilsberg, it is not proved to me that we can at once win our case. It must go before three tribunals in succession. I must think such a matter over with a clear head; it is quite exceptional."

"Oh," said the Colonel, coldly, with a haughty jerk of his head, "if I fail, I can die—but not alone."

The feeble old man had vanished. The eyes were those of a man of energy, lighted up with the spark of desire and revenge.

"We must perhaps compromise," said the lawyer.

"Compromise!" echoed Colonel Chabert. "Am I dead, or am I alive?"

"I hope, monsieur," the attorney went on, "that you will follow my advice. Your cause is mine. You will soon perceive the interest I take in your situation, almost unexampled in judicial records. For the moment I will give you a letter to my notary, who will pay to your order fifty francs every ten days. It would be unbecoming for you to come here to receive alms. If you are Colonel Chabert, you ought to be at no man's mercy. I shall record these advances as a loan; you have estates to recover; you are rich."

This delicate compassion brought tears to the old man's eyes. Derville rose hastily, for it was perhaps not correct for a lawyer to show emotion; he went into the adjoining room, and came back with an unsealed letter, which he gave to the Colonel. When the poor man held it in his hand, he felt through the paper two gold pieces.

"Will you be good enough to describe the documents, and tell me the name of the town, and in what kingdom?" said the lawyer.

The Colonel dictated the information, and verified the spelling of the names of places; then he took his hat in one hand, looked at Derville, and held out the other—a horny hand, saying with much simplicity:

"On my honor, sir, after the Emperor, you are the man to whom I shall owe most. You are a splendid fellow!"

The attorney clapped his hand into the Colonel's, saw him to the stairs, and held a light for him.

"Boucard," said Derville to his head clerk, "I have just listened to a tale that may cost me five and twenty louis. If I am robbed, I shall not regret the money, for I shall have seen the most consummate actor of the day."

When the Colonel was in the street and close to a lamp, he took the two twenty-franc pieces out of the letter and looked at them for a moment under the light. It was the first gold he had seen for nine years.

"I may smoke cigars!" he said to himself.

About three months after this interview, at night, in Derville's room, the notary commissioned to advance the half-pay on Derville's account to his eccentric client, came to consult the attorney on a serious matter, and began by begging him to refund the six hundred francs that the old soldier had received.

"Are you amusing yourself with pensioning the old army?" said the notary, laughing—a young man named Crottat, who had just bought up the office in which he had been head clerk, his chief having fled in consequence of a disastrous bankruptcy.

"I have to thank you, my dear sir, for reminding me of that affair," replied Derville. "My philanthropy will not carry me beyond twenty-five louis; I have, I fear, already been the dupe of my patriotism."

As Derville finished the sentence, he saw on his desk the papers his head clerk had laid out for him. His eye was struck by the appearance of the stamps—long, square, and triangular, in red and blue ink, which distinguished a letter that had come through the Prussian, Austrian, Bavarian, and French post-offices.

"Ah ha!" said he with a laugh, "here is the last act of the comedy; now we shall see if I have been taken in!"

He took up the letter and opened it; but he could not read it; it was written in German.

"Boucard, go yourself and have this letter translated, and bring it back immediately," said Derville, half opening his study door, and giving the letter to the head clerk.

The notary at Berlin, to whom the lawyer had written, informed him that the documents he had been requested to forward would arrive within a few days of this note announcing them. They were, he said, all perfectly regular and duly witnessed, and legally stamped to serve as evidence in law. He also informed him that almost all the witnesses to the facts recorded under these affidavits were still to be found at Eylau, in Prussia, and that the woman to whom M. le Comte Chabert owed his life was still living in a suburb of Heilsberg.

"This looks like business," cried Derville, when Boucard had given him the substance of the letter. "But look here, my boy," he went on, addressing the notary, "I shall want some information which ought to exist in your office. Was it not that old rascal Roguin—?"

"We will say that unfortunate, that ill-used Roguin," interrupted Alexandre Crottat with a laugh.

"Well, was it not that ill-used man who has just carried off eight hundred thousand francs of his clients' money, and reduced several families to despair, who effected the settlement of Chabert's estate? I fancy I have seen that in the documents in our case of Ferraud."

"Yes," said Crottat. "It was when I was third clerk; I copied the papers and studied them thoroughly. Rose Chapotel, wife and widow of Hyacinthe, called Chabert, Count of the Empire, grand officer of the Legion of Honor. They had married without settlement; thus, they held all the property in common. To the best of my recollections, the personalty was about six hundred thousand francs. Before his marriage, Colonel Chabert had made a will in favor of the hospitals of Paris, by which he left them one-quarter of the fortune he might possess at the time of his decease, the State to take the other quarter. The will was contested, there was a forced sale, and then a division, for the attorneys went at a pace. At the time of the settlement the monster who was then governing France handed over to the widow, by special decree, the portion bequeathed to the treasury."

"So that Comte Chabert's personal fortune was no more than three hundred thousand francs?"

"Consequently so it was, old fellow!" said Crottat. "You lawyers sometimes are very clear-headed, though you are accused of false practices in pleading for one side or the other."

Colonel Chabert, whose address was written at the bottom of the first receipt he had given the notary, was lodging in the Faubourg Saint-Marceau, Rue du Petit-Banquier, with an old quartermaster of the Imperial Guard, now a cowkeeper, named Vergniaud. Having reached the spot, Derville was obliged to go on foot in search of his client, for his coachman declined to drive along an unpaved street, where the ruts were rather too deep for cab wheels. Looking about him on all sides, the lawyer at last discovered at the end of the street nearest to the boulevard, between two walls built of bones and mud, two shabby stone gate-posts, much knocked about by carts, in spite of two wooden stumps that served as blocks. These posts supported a cross beam with a penthouse coping of tiles, and on the beam, in red letters, were the words, "Vergniaud, dairyman." To the right of this inscription were some eggs, to the left a cow, all painted in white. The gate was open, and no doubt remained open all day. Beyond a good-sized yard there was a house facing the gate, if indeed the name of house may be applied to one of the hovels built in the neighborhood of Paris, which are like nothing else, not even the most wretched dwellings in the country, of which they have all the poverty without their poetry.

Indeed, in the midst of the fields, even a hovel may have a certain grace derived from the pure air, the verdure, the open country—a hill, a serpentine road, vineyards, quickset hedges, moss-grown thatch and rural implements; but poverty in Paris gains dignity only by horror. Though recently built, this house seemed ready to fall into ruins. None of its materials had found a legitimate use; they had been collected from the various demolitions which are going on every day in Paris. On a shutter made of the boards of a shop-sign Derville read the words, "Fancy Goods." The windows were all mismatched and grotesquely placed. The ground floor, which seemed to be the habitable part, was on one side raised above the soil, and on the other sunk in the rising ground. Between the gate and the house lay a puddle full of stable litter, into which flowed the rain-water and house waste. The back wall of this frail construction, which seemed rather more solidly built than the rest, supported a row of barred hutches, where rabbits bred their numerous families. To the right of the gate was the cowhouse, with a loft above for fodder; it communicated with the house through the dairy. To the left was a poultry yard, with a stable and pig-styes, the roofs finished, like that of the house, with rough deal boards nailed so as to overlap, and shabbily thatched with rushes.

Like most of the places where the elements of the huge meal daily devoured by Paris are every day prepared, the yard Derville now entered showed traces of the hurry that comes of the necessity for being ready at a fixed hour. The large pot-bellied tin cans in which milk is carried, and the little pots for cream, were flung pell-mell at the dairy door, with their linen-covered stoppers. The rags that were used to clean them, fluttered in the sunshine, riddled with holes, hanging to strings fastened to poles. The placid horse, of a breed known only to milk-women, had gone a few steps from the cart, and was standing in front of the stable, the door being shut. A goat was munching the shoots of a starved and dusty vine that clung to the cracked yellow wall of the house. A cat, squatting on the cream jars, was licking them over. The fowls, scared by Derville's approach, scuttered away screaming, and the watch-dog barked.

"And the man who decided the victory at Eylau is to be found here!" said Derville to himself, as his eyes took in at a glance the general effect of the squalid scene.

The house had been left in charge of three little boys. One, who had climbed to the top of the cart loaded with hay, was pitching stones into the chimney of a neighboring house, in the hope that they might fall into a saucepan; another was trying to get a pig into a cart, to hoist it by making the whole thing tilt. When Derville asked them if M. Chabert lived there, neither of them replied, but all three looked at him with a sort of bright stupidity, if I may combine those two words. Derville repeated his questions, but without success. Provoked by the saucy cunning of these three imps, he abused them with the sort of pleasantry which young men think they have the right to address to little boys, and they broke the silence with a horse-laugh. Then Derville was angry.

The Colonel, hearing him, now came out of the little low room, close to the dairy, and stood on the threshold of his doorway with indescribable military coolness. He had in his mouth a very finely-colored pipe—a technical phrase to a smoker—a humble, short clay pipe of the kind called "*brule-queule*." He lifted the peak of a dreadfully greasy cloth cap, saw Derville, and came straight across the midden to join his benefactor the sooner, calling out in friendly tones to the boys:

"Silence in the ranks!"

The children at once kept a respectful silence, which showed the power the old soldier had over them.

"Why did you not write to me?" he said to Derville. "Go along by the cowhouse! There—the path is paved there," he exclaimed, seeing the lawyer's hesitancy, for he did not wish to wet his feet in the manure heap.

Jumping from one dry spot to another, Derville reached the door by which the Colonel had come out. Chabert seemed but ill pleased at having to receive him in the bed-room he occupied; and, in fact, Derville found but one chair there. The Colonel's bed consisted of some trusses of straw, over which his hostess had spread two or three of those old fragments of carpet, picked up heaven knows where, which milk-women use to cover the seats of their carts. The floor was simply the trodden earth. The walls, sweating salt-petre, green with mould, and full of cracks, were so excessively damp that on the side where the Colonel's bed was a reed mat had been nailed. The famous box-coat hung on a nail. Two pairs of old boots lay in a corner. There was not a sign of linen. On the worm-eaten table the *Bulletins de la Grande Armee*, reprinted by Plancher, lay open, and seemed to be the Colonel's reading; his countenance was calm and serene in the midst of this squalor. His visit to Derville seemed to have altered his features; the lawyer perceived in them traces of a happy feeling, a particular gleam set there by hope.

"Does the smell of the pipe annoy you?" he said, placing the dilapidated straw-bottomed chair for his lawyer.

"But, Colonel, you are dreadfully uncomfortable here!"

The speech was wrung from Derville by the distrust natural to lawyers, and the deplorable experience which they derive early in life from the appalling and obscure tragedies at which they look on.

"Here," said he to himself, "is a man who has of course spent my money in satisfying a trooper's three theological virtues—play, wine, and women!"

"To be sure, monsieur, we are not distinguished for luxury here. It is a camp lodging, tempered by friendship, but—" And the soldier shot a deep glance at the man of law—"I have done no one wrong, I have never turned my back on anybody, and I sleep in peace."

Derville reflected that there would be some want of delicacy in asking his client to account for the sums of money he had advanced, so he merely said:

"But why would you not come to Paris, where you might have lived as cheaply as you do here, but where you would have been better lodged?"

"Why," replied the Colonel, "the good folks with whom I am living had taken me in and fed me *gratis* for a year. How could I leave them just when I had a little money? Besides, the father of those three pickles is an old *Egyptian*—"

"An Egyptian!"

"We give that name to the troopers who came back from the expedition into Egypt, of which I was one. Not merely are all who get back brothers; Vergniaud was in my regiment. We have shared a draught of water in the desert; and besides, I have not yet finished teaching his brats to read."

"He might have lodged you better for your money," said Derville.

"Bah!" said the Colonel, "his children sleep on the straw as I do. He and his wife have no better bed; they are very poor you see. They have taken a bigger business than they can manage. But if I recover my fortune... However, it does very well."

"Colonel, to-morrow or the next day, I shall receive your papers from Heilsberg. The woman who dug you out is still alive!"

"Curse the money! To think I haven't got any!" he cried, flinging his pipe on the ground.

Now, a well-colored pipe is to a smoker a precious possession; but the impulse was so natural, the emotion so generous, that every smoker, and the excise office itself, would have pardoned this crime of treason to tobacco. Perhaps the angels may have picked up the pieces.

"Colonel, it is an exceedingly complicated business," said Derville as they left the room to walk up and down in the sunshine.

"To me," said the soldier, "it appears exceedingly simple. I was thought to be dead, and here I am! Give me back my wife and my fortune; give me the rank of General, to which I have a right, for I was made Colonel of the Imperial Guard the day before the battle of Eylau."

"Things are not done so in the legal world," said Derville. "Listen to me. You are Colonel Chabert, I am glad to think it; but it has to be proved judicially to persons whose interest it will be to deny it. Hence, your papers will be disputed. That contention will give rise to ten or twelve preliminary inquiries. Every question will be sent under contradiction up to the supreme court, and give rise to so many costly suits, which will hang on for a long time, however eagerly I may push them. Your opponents will demand an inquiry, which we cannot refuse, and which may necessitate the sending of a commission of investigation to Prussia. But even if we hope for the best; supposing that justice should at once recognize you as Colonel Chabert—can we know how the questions will be settled that will arise out of the very innocent bigamy committed by the Comtesse Ferraud?

"In your case, the point of law is unknown to the Code, and can only be decided as a point in equity, as a jury decides in the delicate cases presented by the social eccentricities of some criminal prosecutions. Now, you had no children by your marriage; M. le Comte Ferraud has two. The judges might pronounce against the marriage where the family ties are weakest, to the confirmation of that where they are stronger, since it was contracted in perfect good faith. Would you be in a very becoming moral position if you insisted, at your age, and in your present circumstances, in resuming your rights over a woman who no longer loves you? You will have both your wife and her husband against you, two important persons who might influence the Bench. Thus, there are many elements which would prolong the case; you will have time to grow old in the bitterest regrets."

"And my fortune?"

"Do you suppose you had a fine fortune?"

"Had I not thirty thousand francs a year?"

"My dear Colonel, in 1799 you made a will before your marriage, leaving one-quarter of your property to hospitals."

"That is true."

"Well, when you were reported dead, it was necessary to make a valuation, and have a sale, to give this quarter away. Your wife was not particular about honesty as to the poor. The valuation, in which she no doubt took care not to include the ready money or jewelry, or too much of the plate, and in which the furniture would be estimated at two-thirds of its actual cost, either to benefit her, or to lighten the succession duty, and also because a valuer can be held responsible for the declared value—the valuation thus made stood at six hundred thousand francs. Your wife had a right of half for her share. Everything was sold and bought in by her; she got something out of it all, and the hospitals got their seventy-five thousand francs. Then, as the remainder went to the State, since you had made no mention of your wife in your will, the Emperor restored to your widow by decree the residue which would have reverted to the Exchequer. So, now, what can you claim? Three hundred thousand francs, no more, and minus the costs."

"And you call that justice!" said the Colonel, in dismay.

"Why, certainly—"

"A pretty kind of justice!"

"So it is, my dear Colonel. You see, that what you thought so easy is not so. Madame Ferraud might even choose to keep the sum given to her by the Emperor."

"But she was not a widow. The decree is utterly void—"

"I agree with you. But every case can get a hearing. Listen to me. I think that under these circumstances a compromise would be both for her and for you the best solution of the question. You will gain by it a more considerable sum than you can prove a right to."

"That would be to sell my wife!"

"With twenty-four thousand francs a year you could find a woman who, in the position in which you are, would suit you better than your own wife, and make you happier. I propose going this very day to see the Comtesse Ferraud and sounding the ground; but I would not take such a step without giving you due notice."

"Let us go together."

"What, just as you are?" said the lawyer. "No, my dear Colonel, no. You might lose your case on the spot."

"Can I possibly gain it?"

"On every count," replied Derville. "But, my dear Colonel Chabert, you overlook one thing. I am not rich; the price of my connection is not wholly paid up. If the bench should allow you a maintenance, that is to say, a sum advanced on your prospects, they will not do so till you have proved that you are Comte Chabert, grand officer of the Legion of Honor."

"To be sure, I am a grand officer of the Legion of Honor; I had forgotten that," said he simply.

"Well, until then," Derville went on, "will you not have to engage pleaders, to have documents copied, to keep the underlings of the law going, and to support yourself? The expenses of the preliminary inquiries will, at a rough guess, amount to ten or twelve thousand francs. I have not so much to lend you—I am crushed as it is by the enormous interest I have to pay on the money I borrowed to buy my business; and you?—Where can you find it."

Large tears gathered in the poor veteran's faded eyes, and rolled down his withered cheeks. This outlook of difficulties discouraged him. The social and the legal world weighed on his breast like a nightmare.

"I will go to the foot of the Vendome column!" he cried. "I will call out: 'I am Colonel Chabert who rode through the Russian square at Eylau!'—The statue—he—he will know me."

"And you will find yourself in Charenton."

At this terrible name the soldier's transports collapsed.

"And will there be no hope for me at the Ministry of War?"

"The war office!" said Derville. "Well, go there; but take a formal legal opinion with you, nullifying the certificate of your death. The government offices would be only too glad if they could annihilate the men of the Empire."

The Colonel stood for a while, speechless, motionless, his eyes fixed, but seeing nothing, sunk in bottomless despair. Military justice is ready and swift; it decides with Turk-like finality, and almost always rightly. This was the only justice known to Chabert. As he saw the labyrinth of difficulties into which he must plunge, and how much money would be required for the journey, the poor old soldier was mortally hit in that power peculiar to man, and called the Will. He thought it would be impossible to live as party to a lawsuit; it seemed a thousand times simpler to remain poor and a beggar, or to enlist as a trooper if any regiment would pass him.

His physical and mental sufferings had already impaired his bodily health in some of the most important organs. He was on the verge of one of those maladies for which medicine has no name, and of which the seat is in some degree variable, like the nervous system itself, the part most frequently attacked of the whole human machine, a malady which may be designated as the heart-sickness of the unfortunate. However serious this invisible but real disorder might already be, it could still be cured by a happy issue. But a fresh obstacle, an unexpected incident, would be enough to wreck this vigorous constitution, to break the weakened springs, and produce the hesitancy, the aimless, unfinished movements, which physiologists know well in men undermined by grief.

Derville, detecting in his client the symptoms of extreme dejection, said to him:

"Take courage; the end of the business cannot fail to be in your favor. Only, consider whether you can give me your whole confidence and blindly accept the result I may think best for your interests."

"Do what you will," said Chabert.

"Yes, but you surrender yourself to me like a man marching to his death."

"Must I not be left to live without a position, without a name? Is that endurable?"

"That is not my view of it," said the lawyer. "We will try a friendly suit, to annul both your death certificate and your marriage, so as to put you in possession of your rights. You may even, by Comte Ferraud's intervention, have your name replaced on the army list as general, and no doubt you will get a pension."

"Well, proceed then," said Chabert. "I put myself entirely in your hands."

"I will send you a power of attorney to sign," said Derville. "Good-bye. Keep up your courage. If you want money, rely on me."

Chabert warmly wrung the lawyer's hand, and remained standing with his back against the wall, not having the energy to follow him excepting with his eyes. Like all men who know but little of legal matters, he was frightened by this unforeseen struggle.

During their interview, several times, the figure of a man posted in the street had come forward from behind one of the gate-pillars, watching for Derville to depart, and he now accosted the lawyer. He was an old man, wearing a blue waistcoat and a white-pleated kilt, like a brewer's; on his head was an otter-skin cap. His face was tanned, hollow-cheeked, and wrinkled, but ruddy on the cheek-bones by hard work and exposure to the open air.

"Asking your pardon, sir," said he, taking Derville by the arm, "if I take the liberty of speaking to you. But I fancied, from the look of you, that you were a friend of our General's."

"And what then?" replied Derville. "What concern have you with him?—But who are you?" said the cautious lawyer.

"I am Louis Vergniaud," he replied at once. "I have a few words to say to you."

"So you are the man who has lodged Comte Chabert as I have found him?"

"Asking your pardon, sir, he has the best room. I would have given him mine if I had had but one; I could have slept in the stable. A man who has suffered as he has, who teaches my kids to read, a general, an Egyptian, the first lieutenant I ever served under—What do you think?—Of us all, he is best served. I shared what I had with him. Unfortunately, it is not much to boast of—bread, milk, eggs. Well, well; it's neighbors' fare, sir. And he is heartily welcome.—But he has hurt our feelings."

"He?"

"Yes, sir, hurt our feelings. To be plain with you, I have taken a larger business than I can manage, and he saw it. Well, it worried him; he must needs mind the horse! I says to him, 'Really, General—' 'Bah!' says he, 'I am not going to eat my head off doing nothing. I learned to rub a horse down many a year ago.'—I had some bills out for the purchase money of my dairy—a fellow named Grados—Do you know him, sir?"

"But, my good man, I have not time to listen to your story. Only tell me how the Colonel offended you."

"He hurt our feelings, sir, as sure as my name is Louis Vergniaud, and my wife cried about it. He heard from our neighbors that we had not a sou to begin to meet the bills with. The old soldier, as he is, he saved up all you gave him, he watched for the bill to come in, and he paid it. Such a trick! While my wife and me, we knew he had no tobacco, poor old boy, and went without.—Oh! now—yes, he has his cigar every morning! I would sell my soul for it—No, we are hurt. Well, so I wanted to ask you—for he said you were a good sort—to lend us a hundred crowns on the stock, so that we may get him some clothes, and furnish his room. He thought he was getting us out of debt, you see? Well, it's just the other way; the old man is running us into debt—and hurt our feelings!—He ought not to have stolen a march on us like that. And we his friends, too!—On my word as an honest man, as sure as my name is Louis Vergniaud, I would sooner sell up and enlist than fail to pay you back your money—"

Derville looked at the dairyman, and stepped back a few paces to glance at the house, the yard, the manure-pool, the cowhouse, the rabbits, the children.

"On my honor, I believe it is characteristic of virtue to have nothing to do with riches!" thought he.

"All right, you shall have your hundred crowns, and more. But I shall not give them to you; the Colonel will be rich enough to help, and I will not deprive him of the pleasure."

"And will that be soon?"

"Why, yes."

"Ah, dear God! how glad my wife will be!" and the cowkeeper's tanned face seemed to expand.

"Now," said Derville to himself, as he got into his cab again, "let us call on our opponent. We must not show our hand, but try to see hers, and win the game at one stroke. She must be frightened. She is a woman. Now, what frightens women most? A woman is afraid of nothing but..."

And he set to work to study the Countess' position, falling into one of those brown studies to which great politicians give themselves up when concocting their own plans and trying to guess the secrets of a hostile Cabinet. Are not attorneys, in a way, statesmen in charge of private affairs?

But a brief survey of the situation in which the Comte Ferraud and his wife now found themselves is necessary for a comprehension of the lawyer's cleverness.

Monsieur le Comte Ferraud was the only son of a former Councillor in the old *Parlement* of Paris, who had emigrated during the Reign of Terror, and so, though he saved his head, lost his fortune. He came back under the Consulate, and remained persistently faithful to the cause of Louis XVIII., in whose circle his father had moved before the Revolution. He thus was one of the party in the Faubourg Saint-Germain which nobly stood out against Napoleon's blandishments. The reputation for capacity gained by the young Count—then simply called Monsieur Ferraud—made him the object of the Emperor's advances, for he was often as well pleased at his conquests among the aristocracy as at gaining a battle. The Count was promised the restitution of his title, of such of his estates as had not been sold, and he was shown in perspective a place in the ministry or as senator.

The Emperor fell.

At the time of Comte Chabert's death, M. Ferraud was a young man of six-and-twenty, without a fortune, of pleasing appearance, who had had his successes, and whom the Faubourg Saint-Germain had adopted as doing it credit; but Madame la Comtesse Chabert had managed to turn her share of her husband's fortune to such good account that, after eighteen months of widowhood, she had about forty thousand francs a year. Her marriage to the young

Count was not regarded as news in the circles of the Faubourg Saint-Germain. Napoleon, approving of this union, which carried out his idea of fusion, restored to Madame Chabert the money falling to the Exchequer under her husband's will; but Napoleon's hopes were again disappointed. Madame Ferraud was not only in love with her lover; she had also been fascinated by the notion of getting into the haughty society which, in spite of its humiliation, was still predominant at the Imperial Court. By this marriage all her vanities were as much gratified as her passions. She was to become a real fine lady. When the Faubourg Saint-Germain understood that the young Count's marriage did not mean desertion, its drawing-rooms were thrown open to his wife.

Then came the Restoration. The Count's political advancement was not rapid. He understood the exigencies of the situation in which Louis XVIII. found himself; he was one of the inner circle who waited till the "Gulf of Revolution should be closed"—for this phrase of the King's, at which the Liberals laughed so heartily, had a political sense. The order quoted in the long lawyer's preamble at the beginning of this story had, however, put him in possession of two tracts of forest, and of an estate which had considerably increased in value during its sequestration. At the present moment, though Comte Ferraud was a Councillor of State, and a Director-General, he regarded his position as merely the first step of his political career.

Wholly occupied as he was by the anxieties of consuming ambition, he had attached to himself, as secretary, a ruined attorney named Delbecq, a more than clever man, versed in all the resources of the law, to whom he left the conduct of his private affairs. This shrewd practitioner had so well understood his position with the Count as to be honest in his own interest. He hoped to get some place by his master's influence, and he made the Count's fortune his first care. His conduct so effectually gave the lie to his former life, that he was regarded as a slandered man. The Countess, with the tact and shrewdness of which most women have a share more or less, understood the man's motives, watched him quietly, and managed him so well, that she had made good use of him for the augmentation of her private fortune. She had contrived to make Delbecq believe that she ruled her husband, and had promised to get him appointed President of an inferior court in some important provincial town, if he devoted himself entirely to her interests.

The promise of a place, not dependent on changes of ministry, which would allow of his marrying advantageously, and rising subsequently to a high political position, by being chosen Depute, made Delbecq the Countess' abject slave. He had never allowed her to miss one of those favorable chances which the fluctuations of the Bourse and the increased value of property afforded to clever financiers in Paris during the first three years after the Restoration. He had trebled his protectress' capital, and all the more easily because the Countess had no scruples as to the means which might make her an enormous fortune as quickly as possible. The emoluments derived by the Count from the places he held she spent on the housekeeping, so as to reinvest her dividends; and Delbecq lent himself to these calculations of avarice without trying to account for her motives. People of that sort never trouble themselves about any secrets of which the discovery is not necessary to their own interests. And, indeed, he naturally found the reason in the thirst for money, which taints almost every Parisian woman; and as a fine fortune was needed to support the pretensions of Comte Ferraud, the secretary sometimes fancied that he saw in the Countess' greed a consequence of her devotion to a husband with whom she still was in love. The Countess buried the secrets of her conduct at the bottom of her heart. There lay the secrets of life and death to her, there lay the turning-point of this history.

At the beginning of the year 1818 the Restoration was settled on an apparently immovable foundation; its doctrines of government, as understood by lofty minds, seemed calculated to bring to France an era of renewed prosperity, and Parisian society changed its aspect. Madame la Comtesse Ferraud found that by chance she had achieved for love a marriage that had brought her fortune and gratified ambition. Still young and handsome, Madame Ferraud played the part of a woman of fashion, and lived in the atmosphere of the Court. Rich herself, with a rich husband who was cried up as one of the ablest men of the royalist party, and, as a friend of the King, certain to be made Minister, she belonged to the aristocracy, and shared its magnificence. In the midst of this triumph she was attacked by a moral canker. There are feelings which women guess in spite of the care men take to bury them. On the first return of the King, Comte Ferraud had begun to regret his marriage. Colonel Chabert's widow had not been the means of allying him to anybody; he was alone and unsupported in steering his way in a course full of shoals and beset by enemies. Also, perhaps, when he came to judge his wife coolly, he may have discerned in her certain vices of education which made her unfit to second him in his schemes.

A speech he made, *a propos* of Talleyrand's marriage, enlightened the Countess, to whom it proved that if he had still been a free man she would never have been Madame Ferraud. What woman could forgive this repentance? Does it not include the germs of every insult, every crime, every form of repudiation? But what a wound must it have left in the Countess' heart, supposing that she lived in the dread of her first husband's return? She had known that he still lived, and she had ignored him. Then during the time when she had heard no more of him, she had chosen to believe that he had fallen at Waterloo with the Imperial Eagle, at the same time as Boutin. She resolved, nevertheless, to bind the Count to her by the strongest of all ties, by a chain of gold, and vowed to be so rich that her fortune might make her second marriage dissoluble, if by chance Colonel Chabert should ever reappear. And he had reappeared; and she could not explain to herself why the struggle she had dreaded had not already begun. Suffering, sickness, had perhaps delivered her from that man. Perhaps he was half mad, and Charenton might yet do her justice. She had not chosen to take either Delbecq or the police into her confidence, for fear of putting herself in their power, or of hastening the catastrophe. There are in Paris many women who, like the Countess Ferraud, live with an unknown moral monster, or on the brink of an abyss; a callus forms over the spot that tortures them, and they can still laugh and enjoy themselves.

"There is something very strange in Comte Ferraud's position," said Derville to himself, on emerging from his long reverie, as his cab stopped at the door of the Hotel Ferraud in the Rue de Varennes. "How is it that he, so rich as he is, and such a favorite with the King, is not yet a peer of France? It may, to be sure, be true that the King, as Mme. de Grandlieu was telling me, desires to keep up the value of the *pairie* by not bestowing it right and left. And, after all, the son of a Councillor of the *Parlement* is not a Crillon nor a Rohan. A Comte Ferraud can only get into the Upper Chamber surreptitiously. But if his marriage were annulled, could he not get the dignity of some old peer who has only daughters transferred to himself, to the King's great satisfaction? At any rate this will be a good bogey to put forward and frighten the Countess," thought he as he went up the steps.

Derville had without knowing it laid his finger on the hidden wound, put his hand on the canker that consumed Madame Ferraud.

She received him in a pretty winter dining-room, where she was at breakfast, while playing with a monkey tethered by a chain to a little pole with climbing bars of iron. The Countess was in an elegant wrapper; the curls of her hair, carelessly pinned up, escaped from a cap, giving her an arch look. She was fresh and smiling. Silver, gilding, and mother-of-pearl shone on the table, and all about the room were rare plants growing in magnificent china jars. As he saw Colonel Chabert's wife, rich with his spoil, in the lap of luxury and the height of fashion, while he, poor wretch, was living with a poor dairyman among the beasts, the lawyer said to himself:

"The moral of all this is that a pretty woman will never acknowledge as her husband, nor even as a lover, a man in an old box-coat, a tow wig, and boots with holes in them."

A mischievous and bitter smile expressed the feelings, half philosophical and half satirical, which such a man was certain to experience—a man well situated to know the truth of things in spite of the lies behind which most families in Paris hide their mode of life.

"Good-morning, Monsieur Derville," said she, giving the monkey some coffee to drink.

"Madame," said he, a little sharply, for the light tone in which she spoke jarred on him. "I have come to speak with you on a very serious matter."

"I am so *grieved*, M. le Comte is away——"

"I, madame, am delighted. It would be grievous if he could be present at our interview. Besides, I am informed through M. Delbecq that you like to manage your own business without troubling the Count."

"Then I will send for Delbecq," said she.

"He would be of no use to you, clever as he is," replied Derville. "Listen to me, madame; one word will be enough to make you grave. Colonel Chabert is alive!"

"Is it by telling me such nonsense as that that you think you can make me grave?" said she with a shout of laughter. But she was suddenly quelled by the singular penetration of the fixed gaze which Derville turned on her, seeming to read to the bottom of her soul.

"Madame," he said with cold and piercing solemnity, "you know not the extent of the danger that threatens you. I need say nothing of the indisputable authenticity of the evidence nor of the fulness of proof which testifies to the identity of Comte Chabert. I am not, as you know, the man to take up a bad cause. If you resist our proceedings to show that the certificate of death was false, you will lose that first case, and that matter once settled, we shall gain every point."

"What, then, do you wish to discuss with me?"

"Neither the Colonel nor yourself. Nor need I allude to the briefs which clever advocates may draw up when armed with the curious facts of this case, or the advantage they may derive from the letters you received from your first husband before your marriage to your second."

"It is false," she cried, with the violence of a spoilt woman. "I never had a letter from Comte Chabert; and if some one is pretending to be the Colonel, it is some swindler, some returned convict, like Coignard perhaps. It makes me shudder only to think of it. Can the Colonel rise from the dead, monsieur? Bonaparte sent an aide-de-camp to inquire for me on his death, and to this day I draw the pension of three thousand francs granted to this widow by the Government. I have been perfectly in the right to turn away all the Chaberts who have ever come, as I shall all who may come."

"Happily we are alone, madame. We can tell lies at our ease," said he coolly, and finding it amusing to lash up the Countess' rage so as to lead her to betray herself, by tactics familiar to lawyers, who are accustomed to keep cool when their opponents or their clients are in a passion. "Well, then, we must fight it out," thought he, instantly hitting on a plan to entrap her and show her her weakness.

"The proof that you received the first letter, madame, is that it contained some securities—"

"Oh, as to securities—that it certainly did not."

"Then you received the letter," said Derville, smiling. "You are caught, madame, in the first snare laid for you by an attorney, and you fancy you could fight against Justice—"

The Countess colored, and then turned pale, hiding her face in her hands. Then she shook off her shame, and retorted with the natural impertinence of such women, "Since you are the so-called Chabert's attorney, be so good as to—"

"Madame," said Derville, "I am at this moment as much your lawyer as I am Colonel Chabert's. Do you suppose I want to lose so valuable a client as you are?—But you are not listening."

"Nay, speak on, monsieur," said she graciously.

"Your fortune came to you from M. le Comte Chabert, and you cast him off. Your fortune is immense, and you leave him to beg. An advocate can be very eloquent when a cause is eloquent in itself; there are here circumstances which might turn public opinion strongly against you."

"But, monsieur," said the Comtesse, provoked by the way in which Derville turned and laid her on the gridiron, "even if I grant that your M. Chabert is living, the law will uphold my second marriage on account of the children, and I shall get off with the restitution of two hundred and twenty-five thousand francs to M. Chabert."

"It is impossible to foresee what view the Bench may take of the question. If on one side we have a mother and children, on the other we have an old man crushed by sorrows, made old by your refusals to know him. Where is he to find a wife? Can the judges contravene the law? Your marriage with Colonel Chabert has priority on its side and every legal right. But if you appear under disgraceful colors, you might have an unlooked-for adversary. That, madame, is the danger against which I would warn you."

"And who is he?"

"Comte Ferraud."

"Monsieur Ferraud has too great an affection for me, too much respect for the mother of his children—"

"Do not talk of such absurd things," interrupted Derville, "to lawyers, who are accustomed to read hearts to the bottom. At this instant Monsieur Ferraud has not the slightest wish to annual your union, and I am quite sure that he adores you; but if some one were to tell him that his marriage is void, that his wife will be called before the bar of public opinion as a criminal—"

"He would defend me, monsieur."

"No, madame."

"What reason could he have for deserting me, monsieur?"

"That he would be free to marry the only daughter of a peer of France, whose title would be conferred on him by patent from the King."

The Countess turned pale.

"A hit!" said Derville to himself. "I have you on the hip; the poor Colonel's case is won."—"Besides, madame," he went on aloud, "he would feel all the less remorse because a man covered with glory—a General, Count, Grand Cross of the Legion of Honor—is not such a bad alternative; and if that man insisted on his wife's returning to him—"

"Enough, enough, monsieur!" she exclaimed. "I will never have any lawyer but you. What is to be done?"

"Compromise!" said Derville.

"Does he still love me?" she said.

"Well, I do not think he can do otherwise."

The Countess raised her head at these words. A flash of hope shone in her eyes; she thought perhaps that she could speculate on her first husband's affection to gain her cause by some feminine cunning.

"I shall await your orders, madame, to know whether I am to report our proceedings to you, or if you will come to my office to agree to the terms of a compromise," said Derville, taking leave.

A week after Derville had paid these two visits, on a fine morning in June, the husband and wife, who had been separated by an almost supernatural chance, started from the opposite ends of Paris to meet in the office of the lawyer who was engaged by both. The supplies liberally advanced by Derville to Colonel Chabert had enabled him to dress as suited his position in life, and the dead man arrived in a very decent cab. He wore a wig suited to his face, was dressed in blue cloth with white linen, and wore under his waistcoat the broad red ribbon of the higher grade of the Legion of Honor. In resuming the habits of wealth he had recovered his soldierly style. He held himself up; his face, grave and mysterious-looking, reflected his happiness and all his hopes, and seemed to have acquired youth and *impasto*, to borrow a picturesque word from the painter's art. He was no more like the Chabert of the old box-coat than a cartwheel double sou is like a newly coined forty-franc piece. The passer-by, only to see him, would have recognized at once one of the noble wrecks of our old army, one of the heroic men on whom our national glory is reflected, as a splinter of ice on which the sun shines seems to reflect every beam. These veterans are at once a picture and a book.

When the Count jumped out of his carriage to go into Derville's office, he did it as lightly as a young man. Hardly had his cab moved off, when a smart brougham drove up, splendid with coats-of-arms. Madame la Comtesse Ferraud stepped out in a dress which, though simple, was cleverly designed to show how youthful her figure was. She wore a pretty drawn bonnet lined with pink, which framed her face to perfection, softening its outlines and making it look younger.

If the clients were rejuvenescent, the office was unaltered, and presented the same picture as that described at the beginning of this story. Simonnin was eating his breakfast, his shoulder leaning against the window, which was then open, and he was staring up at the blue sky in the opening of the courtyard enclosed by four gloomy houses.

"Ah, ha!" cried the little clerk, "who will bet an evening at the play that Colonel Chabert is a General, and wears a red ribbon?"

"The chief is a great magician," said Godeschal.

"Then there is no trick to play on him this time?" asked Desroches.

"His wife has taken that in hand, the Comtesse Ferraud," said Boucard.

"What next?" said Godeschal. "Is Comtesse Ferraud required to belong to two men?"

"Here she is," answered Simonnin.

"So you are not deaf, you young rogue!" said Chabert, taking the gutter-jumper by the ear and twisting it, to the delight of the other clerks, who began to laugh, looking at the Colonel with the curious attention due to so singular a personage.

Comte Chabert was in Derville's private room at the moment when his wife came in by the door of the office.

"I say, Boucard, there is going to be a queer scene in the chief's room! There is a woman who can spend her days alternately, the odd with Comte Ferraud, and the even with Comte Chabert."

"And in leap year," said Godeschal, "they must settle the *count* between them."

"Silence, gentlemen, you can be heard!" said Boucard severely. "I never was in an office where there was so much jesting as there is here over the clients."

Derville had made the Colonel retire to the bedroom when the Countess was admitted.

"Madame," he said, "not knowing whether it would be agreeable to you to meet M. le Comte Chabert, I have placed you apart. If, however, you should wish it—"

"It is an attention for which I am obliged to you."

"I have drawn up the memorandum of an agreement of which you and M. Chabert can discuss the conditions, here, and now. I will go alternately to him and to you, and explain your views respectively."

"Let me see, monsieur," said the Countess impatiently.

Derville read aloud:

"'Between the undersigned:

"'M. Hyacinthe Chabert, Count, Marechal de Camp, and Grand Officer of the Legion of Honor, living in Paris, Rue du Petit-Banquier, on the one part;

"'And Madame Rose Chapotel, wife of the aforesaid M. le Comte Chabert, *nee*—'"

"Pass over the preliminaries," said she. "Come to the conditions."

"Madame," said the lawyer, "the preamble briefly sets forth the position in which you stand to each other. Then, by the first clause, you acknowledge, in the presence of three witnesses, of whom two shall be notaries, and one the dairyman with whom your husband has been lodging, to all of whom your secret is known, and who will be absolutely silent—you acknowledge, I say, that the individual designated in the documents subjoined to the deed, and whose identity is to be further proved by an act of recognition prepared by your notary, Alexandre Crottat, is your first husband, Comte Chabert. By the second clause Comte Chabert, to secure your happiness, will undertake to assert his rights only under certain circumstances set forth in the deed.—And these," said Derville, in a parenthesis, "are none other than a failure to carry out the conditions of this secret agreement.—M. Chabert, on his part, agrees to accept judgment on a friendly suit, by which his certificate of death shall be annulled, and his marriage dissolved."

"That will not suit me in the least," said the Countess with surprise. "I will be a party to no suit; you know why."

"By the third clause," Derville went on, with imperturbable coolness, "you pledge yourself to secure to Hyacinthe Comte Chabert an income of twenty-four thousand francs on government stock held in his name, to revert to you at his death—"

"But it is much too dear!" exclaimed the Countess.

"Can you compromise the matter cheaper?"

"Possibly."

"But what do you want, madame?"

"I want—I will not have a lawsuit. I want—"

"You want him to remain dead?" said Derville, interrupting her hastily.

"Monsieur," said the Countess, "if twenty-four thousand francs a year are necessary, we will go to law—"

"Yes, we will go to law," said the Colonel in a deep voice, as he opened the door and stood before his wife, with one hand in his waistcoat and the other hanging by his side—an attitude to which the recollection of his adventure gave horrible significance.

"It is he," said the Countess to herself.

"Too dear!" the old soldier exclaimed. "I have given you near on a million, and you are cheapening my misfortunes. Very well; now I will have you—you and your fortune. Our goods are in common, our marriage is not dissolved—"

"But monsieur is not Colonel Chabert!" cried the Countess, in feigned amazement.

"Indeed!" said the old man, in a tone of intense irony. "Do you want proofs? I found you in the Palais Royal—"

The Countess turned pale. Seeing her grow white under her rouge, the old soldier paused, touched by the acute suffering he was inflicting on the woman he had once so ardently loved; but she shot such a venomous glance at him that he abruptly went on:

"You were with La—"

"Allow me, Monsieur Derville," said the Countess to the lawyer. "You must give me leave to retire. I did not come here to listen to such dreadful things."

She rose and went out. Derville rushed after her; but the Countess had taken wings, and seemed to have flown from the place.

On returning to his private room, he found the Colonel in a towering rage, striding up and down.

"In those times a man took his wife where he chose," said he. "But I was foolish and chose badly; I trusted to appearances. She has no heart."

"Well, Colonel, was I not right to beg you not to come?—I am now positive of your identity; when you came in, the Countess gave a little start, of which the meaning was unequivocal. But you have lost your chances. Your wife knows that you are unrecognizable."

"I will kill her!"

"Madness! you will be caught and executed like any common wretch. Besides you might miss! That would be unpardonable. A man must not miss his shot when he wants to kill his wife.— Let me set things straight; you are only a big child. Go now. Take care of yourself; she is capable of setting some trap for you and shutting you up in Charenton. I will notify her of our proceedings to protect you against a surprise."

The unhappy Colonel obeyed his young benefactor, and went away, stammering apologies. He slowly went down the dark staircase, lost in gloomy thoughts, and crushed perhaps by the blow just dealt him—the most cruel he could feel, the thrust that could most deeply pierce his heart—when he heard the rustle of a woman's dress on the lowest landing, and his wife stood before him.

"Come, monsieur," said she, taking his arm with a gesture like those familiar to him of old. Her action and the accent of her voice, which had recovered its graciousness, were enough to allay the Colonel's wrath, and he allowed himself to be led to the carriage.

"Well, get in!" said she, when the footman had let down the step.

And as if by magic, he found himself sitting by his wife in the brougham.

"Where to?" asked the servant.

"To Groslay," said she.

The horses started at once, and carried them all across Paris.

"Monsieur," said the Countess, in a tone of voice which betrayed one of those emotions which are rare in our lives, and which agitate every part of our being. At such moments the heart, fibres, nerves, countenance, soul, and body, everything, every pore even, feels a thrill. Life no longer seems to be within us; it flows out, springs forth, is communicated as if by contagion, transmitted by a look, a tone of voice, a gesture, impressing our will on others. The old soldier started on hearing this single word, this first, terrible "monsieur!" But still it was at once a reproach and a pardon, a hope and a despair, a question and an answer. This word included them all; none but an actress could have thrown so much eloquence, so many feelings into a single word. Truth is less complete in its utterance; it does not put everything on the outside; it allows us to see what is within. The Colonel was filled with remorse for his suspicions, his demands, and his anger; he looked down not to betray his agitation.

"Monsieur," repeated she, after an imperceptible pause, "I knew you at once."

"Rosine," said the old soldier, "those words contain the only balm that can help me to forget my misfortunes."

Two large tears rolled hot on to his wife's hands, which he pressed to show his paternal affection.

"Monsieur," she went on, "could you not have guessed what it cost me to appear before a stranger in a position so false as mine now is? If I have to blush for it, at least let it be in the privacy of my family. Ought not such a secret to remain buried in our hearts? You will forgive me, I hope, for my apparent indifference to the woes of a Chabert in whose existence I could not possibly believe. I received your letters," she hastily added, seeing in his face the objection it expressed, "but they did not reach me till thirteen months after the battle of Eylau. They were opened, dirty, the writing was unrecognizable; and after obtaining Napoleon's signature to my second marriage contract, I could not help believing that some clever swindler wanted to make a fool of me. Therefore, to avoid disturbing Monsieur Ferraud's peace of mind, and disturbing family ties, I was obliged to take precautions against a pretended Chabert. Was I not right, I ask you?"

"Yes, you were right. It was I who was the idiot, the owl, the dolt, not to have calculated better what the consequences of such a position might be.—But where are we going?" he asked, seeing that they had reached the barrier of La Chapelle.

"To my country house near Groslay, in the valley of Montmorency. There, monsieur, we will consider the steps to be taken. I know my duties. Though I am yours by right, I am no longer yours in fact. Can you wish that we should become the talk of Paris? We need not inform the public of a situation, which for me has its ridiculous side, and let us preserve our dignity. You still love me," she said, with a sad, sweet gaze at the Colonel, "but have not I been authorized to form other ties? In so strange a position, a secret voice bids me trust to your kindness, which is so well known to me. Can I be wrong in taking you as the sole arbiter of my fate? Be at once judge and party to the suit. I trust in your noble character; you will be generous enough to forgive me for the consequences of faults committed in innocence. I may then confess to you: I love M. Ferraud. I believed that I had a right to love him. I do not blush to make this confession to you; even if it offends you, it does not disgrace us. I cannot conceal the facts. When fate made me a widow, I was not a mother."

The Colonel with a wave of his hand bid his wife be silent, and for a mile and a half they sat without speaking a single word. Chabert could fancy he saw the two little ones before him.

"Rosine."

"Monsieur?"

"The dead are very wrong to come to life again."

"Oh, monsieur, no, no! Do not think me ungrateful. Only, you find me a lover, a mother, while you left me merely a wife. Though it is no longer in my power to love, I know how much I owe you, and I can still offer you all the affection of a daughter."

"Rosine," said the old man in a softened tone, "I no longer feel any resentment against you. We will forget anything," he added, with one of those smiles which always reflect a noble soul; "I have not so little delicacy as to demand the mockery of love from a wife who no longer loves me."

The Countess gave him a flashing look full of such deep gratitude that poor Chabert would have been glad to sink again into his grave at Eylau. Some men have a soul strong enough for such self-devotion, of which the whole reward consists in the assurance that they have made the person they love happy.

"My dear friend, we will talk all this over later when our hearts have rested," said the Countess.

The conversation turned to other subjects, for it was impossible to dwell very long on this one. Though the couple came back again and again to their singular position, either by some allusion or of serious purpose, they had a delightful drive, recalling the events of their former life together and the times of the Empire. The Countess knew how to lend peculiar charm to her reminiscences, and gave the conversation the tinge of melancholy that was needed to keep it serious. She revived his love without awakening his desires, and allowed her first husband to discern the mental wealth she had acquired while trying to accustom him to moderate his pleasure to that which a father may feel in the society of a favorite daughter.

The Colonel had known the Countess of the Empire; he found her a Countess of the Restoration.

At last, by a cross-road, they arrived at the entrance to a large park lying in the little valley which divides the heights of Margency from the pretty village of Groslay. The Countess had there a delightful house, where the Colonel on arriving found everything in readiness for his stay there, as well as for his wife's. Misfortune is a kind of talisman whose virtue consists in its power to confirm our original nature; in some men it increases their distrust and malignancy, just as it improves the goodness of those who have a kind heart.

Sorrow had made the Colonel even more helpful and good than he had always been, and he could understand some secrets of womanly distress which are unrevealed to most men. Nevertheless, in spite of his loyal trustfulness, he could not help saying to his wife:

"Then you felt quite sure you would bring me here?"

"Yes," replied she, "if I found Colonel Chabert in Derville's client."

The appearance of truth she contrived to give to this answer dissipated the slight suspicions which the Colonel was ashamed to have felt. For three days the Countess was quite charming to her first husband. By tender attentions and unfailing sweetness she seemed anxious to wipe out the memory of the sufferings he had endured, and to earn forgiveness for the woes which, as she confessed, she had innocently caused him. She delighted in displaying for him the charms she knew he took pleasure in, while at the same time she assumed a kind of melancholy; for men are more especially accessible to certain ways, certain graces of the heart or of the mind which they cannot resist. She aimed at interesting him in her position, and appealing to his feelings so far as to take possession of his mind and control him despotically.

Ready for anything to attain her ends, she did not yet know what she was to do with this man; but at any rate she meant to annihilate him socially. On the evening of the third day she felt that in spite of her efforts she could not conceal her uneasiness as to the results of her manoeuvres. To give herself a minute's reprieve she went up to her room, sat down before her writing-table, and laid aside the mask of composure which she wore in Chabert's presence, like an actress who, returning to her dressing-room after a fatiguing fifth act, drops half dead, leaving with the audience an image of herself which she no longer resembles. She proceeded to finish a letter she had begun to Delbecq, whom she desired to go in her name and demand of Derville the deeds relating to Colonel Chabert, to copy them, and to come to her at once to Groslay. She had hardly finished when she heard the Colonel's step in the passage; uneasy at her absence, he had come to look for her.

"Alas!" she exclaimed, "I wish I were dead! My position is

intolerable..."

"Why, what is the matter?" asked the good man.

"Nothing, nothing!" she replied.

She rose, left the Colonel, and went down to speak privately to her maid, whom she sent off to Paris, impressing on her that she was herself to deliver to Delbecq the letter just written, and to bring it back to the writer as soon as he had read it. Then the Countess went out to sit on a bench sufficiently in sight for the Colonel to join her as soon as he might choose. The Colonel, who was looking for her, hastened up and sat down by her.

"Rosine," said he, "what is the matter with you?"

She did not answer.

It was one of those glorious, calm evenings in the month of June, whose secret harmonies infuse such sweetness into the sunset. The air was clear, the stillness perfect, so that far away in the park they could hear the voices of some children, which added a kind of melody to the sublimity of the scene.

"You do not answer me?" the Colonel said to his wife.

"My husband——" said the Countess, who broke off, started a little, and with a blush stopped to ask him, "What am I to say when I speak of M. Ferraud?"

"Call him your husband, my poor child," replied the Colonel, in a kind voice. "Is he not the father of your children?"

"Well, then," she said, "if he should ask what I came here for, if he finds out that I came here, alone, with a stranger, what am I to say to him? Listen, monsieur," she went on, assuming a dignified attitude, "decide my fate, I am resigned to anything——"

"My dear," said the Colonel, taking possession of his wife's hands, "I have made up my mind to sacrifice myself entirely for your happiness——"

"That is impossible!" she exclaimed, with a sudden spasmodic movement. "Remember that you would have to renounce your identity, and in an authenticated form."

"What?" said the Colonel. "Is not my word enough for you?"

The word "authenticated" fell on the old man's heart, and roused involuntary distrust. He looked at his wife in a way that made her color, she cast down her eyes, and he feared that he might find himself compelled to despise her. The Countess was afraid lest she had scared the shy modesty, the stern honesty, of a man whose generous temper and primitive virtues were known to her. Though these feelings had brought the clouds to her brow, they immediately recovered their harmony. This was the way of it. A child's cry was heard in the distance.

"Jules, leave your sister in peace," the Countess called out.

"What, are your children here?" said Chabert.

"Yes, but I told them not to trouble you."

The old soldier understood the delicacy, the womanly tact of so gracious a precaution, and took the Countess' hand to kiss it.

"But let them come," said he.

The little girl ran up to complain of her brother.

"Mamma!"

"Mamma!"

"It was Jules—"

"It was her—"

Their little hands were held out to their mother, and the two childish voices mingled; it was an unexpected and charming picture.

"Poor little things!" cried the Countess, no longer restraining her tears, "I shall have to leave them. To whom will the law assign them? A mother's heart cannot be divided; I want them, I want them."

"Are you making mamma cry?" said Jules, looking fiercely at

the Colonel.

"Silence, Jules!" said the mother in a decided tone.

The two children stood speechless, examining their mother and the stranger with a curiosity which it is impossible to express in words.

"Oh yes!" she cried. "If I am separated from the Count, only leave me my children, and I will submit to anything..."

This was the decisive speech which gained all that she had hoped from it.

"Yes," exclaimed the Colonel, as if he were ending a sentence already begun in his mind, "I must return underground again. I had told myself so already."

"Can I accept such a sacrifice?" replied his wife. "If some men have died to save a mistress' honor, they gave their life but once. But in this case you would be giving your life every day. No, no. It is impossible. If it were only your life, it would be nothing; but to sign a declaration that you are not Colonel Chabert, to acknowledge yourself an imposter, to sacrifice your honor, and live a lie every hour of the day! Human devotion cannot go so far. Only think!— No. But for my poor children I would have fled with you by this time to the other end of the world."

"But," said Chabert, "cannot I live here in your little lodge as one of your relations? I am as worn out as a cracked cannon; I want nothing but a little tobacco and the *Constitutionnel.*"

The Countess melted into tears. There was a contest of generosity between the Comtesse Ferraud and Colonel Chabert, and the soldier came out victorious. One evening, seeing this mother with her children, the soldier was bewitched by the touching grace of a family picture in the country, in the shade and the silence; he made a resolution to remain dead, and, frightened no longer at the authentication of a deed, he asked what he could do to secure beyond all risk the happiness of this family.

"Do exactly as you like," said the Countess. "I declare to you that I will have nothing to do with this affair. I ought not."

Delbecq had arrived some days before, and in obedience to the Countess' verbal instructions, the intendant had succeeded in gaining the old soldier's confidence. So on the following morning Colonel Chabert went with the erewhile attorney to Saint-Leu-Taverny, where Delbecq had caused the notary to draw up an affidavit in such terms that, after hearing it read, the Colonel started up and walked out of the office.

"Turf and thunder! What a fool you must think me! Why, I should make myself out a swindler!" he exclaimed.

"Indeed, monsieur," said Delbecq, "I should advise you not to sign in haste. In your place I would get at least thirty thousand francs a year out of the bargain. Madame would pay them."

After annihilating this scoundrel *emeritus* by the lightning look of an honest man insulted, the Colonel rushed off, carried away by a thousand contrary emotions. He was suspicious, indignant, and calm again by turns.

Finally he made his way back into the park of Groslay by a gap in a fence, and slowly walked on to sit down and rest, and meditate at his ease, in a little room under a gazebo, from which the road to Saint-Leu could be seen. The path being strewn with the yellowish sand which is used instead of river-gravel, the Countess, who was sitting in the upper room of this little summer-house, did not hear the Colonel's approach, for she was too much preoccupied with the success of her business to pay the smallest attention to the slight noise made by her husband. Nor did the old man notice that his wife was in the room over him.

"Well, Monsieur Delbecq, has he signed?" the Countess asked her secretary, whom she saw alone on the road beyond the hedge of a haha.

"No, madame. I do not even know what has become of our man. The old horse reared."

"Then we shall be obliged to put him into Charenton," said she, "since we have got him."

The Colonel, who recovered the elasticity of youth to leap the haha, in the twinkling of an eye was standing in front of Delbecq, on whom he bestowed the two finest slaps that ever a scoundrel's cheeks received.

"And you may add that old horses can kick!" said he.

His rage spent, the Colonel no longer felt vigorous enough to leap the ditch. He had seen the truth in all its nakedness. The Countess' speech and Delbecq's reply had revealed the conspiracy of which he was to be the victim. The care taken of him was but a bait to entrap him in a snare. That speech was like a drop of subtle poison, bringing on in the old soldier a return of all his sufferings, physical and moral. He came back to the summer-house through the park gate, walking slowly like a broken man.

Then for him there was to be neither peace nor truce. From this moment he must begin the odious warfare with this woman of which Derville had spoken, enter on a life of litigation, feed on gall, drink every morning of the cup of bitterness. And then— fearful thought!—where was he to find the money needful to pay the cost of the first proceedings? He felt such disgust of life, that if there had been any water at hand he would have thrown himself into it; that if he had had a pistol, he would have blown out his brains. Then he relapsed into the indecision of mind which, since his conversation with Derville at the dairyman's had changed his character.

At last, having reached the kiosque, he went up to the gazebo, where little rose-windows afforded a view over each lovely landscape of the valley, and where he found his wife seated on a chair. The Countess was gazing at the distance, and preserved a calm countenance, showing that impenetrable face which women can assume when resolved to do their worst. She wiped her eyes as if she had been weeping, and played absently with the pink ribbons of her sash. Nevertheless, in spite of her apparent assurance, she could not help shuddering slightly when she saw before her her venerable benefactor, standing with folded arms, his face pale, his brow stern.

"Madame," he said, after gazing at her fixedly for a moment and compelling her to blush, "Madame, I do not curse you—I scorn you. I can now thank the chance that has divided us. I do not feel even a desire for revenge; I no longer love you. I want nothing from you. Live in peace on the strength of my word; it is worth more than the scrawl of all the notaries in Paris. I will never assert my claim to the name I perhaps have made illustrious. I am henceforth but a poor devil named Hyacinthe, who asks no more than his share of the sunshine.—Farewell!"

The Countess threw herself at his feet; she would have detained him by taking his hands, but he pushed her away with disgust, saying:

"Do not touch me!"

The Countess' expression when she heard her husband's retreating steps is quite indescribable. Then, with the deep perspicacity given only by utter villainy, or by fierce worldly selfishness, she knew that she might live in peace on the word and the contempt of this loyal veteran.

Chabert, in fact, disappeared. The dairyman failed in business, and became a hackney-cab driver. The Colonel, perhaps, took up some similar industry for a time. Perhaps, like a stone flung into a chasm, he went falling from ledge to ledge, to be lost in the mire of rags that seethes through the streets of Paris.

Six months after this event, Derville, hearing no more of Colonel Chabert or the Comtesse Ferraud, supposed that they had no doubt come to a compromise, which the Countess, out of revenge, had had arranged by some other lawyer. So one morning he added up the sums he had advanced to the said Chabert with the costs, and begged the Comtesse Ferraud to claim from M. le Comte Chabert the amount of the bill, assuming that she would know where to find her first husband.

The very next day Comte Ferraud's man of business, lately appointed President of the County Court in a town of some importance, wrote this distressing note to Derville:

"MONSIEUR,—

"Madame la Comtesse Ferraud desires me to inform you that your client took complete advantage of your confidence, and that the individual calling himself Comte Chabert has acknowledged that he came forward under false pretences.

"Yours, etc., DELBECQ."

"One comes across people who are, on my honor, too stupid by half," cried Derville. "They don't deserve to be Christians! Be humane, generous, philanthropical, and a lawyer, and you are bound to be cheated! There is a piece of business that will cost me two thousand-franc notes!"

Some time after receiving this letter, Derville went to the Palais de Justice in search of a pleader to whom he wished to speak, and who was employed in the Police Court. As chance would have it, Derville went into Court Number 6 at the moment when the Presiding Magistrate was sentencing one Hyacinthe to two months' imprisonment as a vagabond, and subsequently to be taken to the Mendicity House of Detention, a sentence which, by magistrates' law, is equivalent to perpetual imprisonment. On hearing the name of Hyacinthe, Derville looked at the deliquent, sitting between two *gendarmes* on the bench for the accused, and recognized in the condemned man his false Colonel Chabert.

The old soldier was placid, motionless, almost absentminded. In spite of his rags, in spite of the misery stamped on his countenance, it gave evidence of noble pride. His eye had a stoical expression which no magistrate ought to have misunderstood; but as soon as a man has fallen into the hands of justice, he is no more than a moral entity, a matter of law or of fact, just as to statists he has become a zero.

When the veteran was taken back to the lock-up, to be removed later with the batch of vagabonds at that moment at the bar, Derville availed himself of the privilege accorded to lawyers of going wherever they please in the Courts, and followed him to the lock-up, where he stood scrutinizing him for some minutes, as well as the curious crew of beggars among whom he found himself. The passage to the lock-up at that moment afforded one of those spectacles which, unfortunately, neither legislators, nor philanthropists, nor painters, nor writers come to study. Like all the laboratories of the law, this ante-room is a dark and malodorous place; along the walls runs a wooden seat, blackened by the constant presence there of the wretches who come to this meeting-place of every form of social squalor, where not one of them is missing.

A poet might say that the day was ashamed to light up this dreadful sewer through which so much misery flows! There is not a spot on that plank where some crime has not sat, in embryo or matured; not a corner where a man has never stood who, driven to despair by the blight which justice has set upon him after his first fault, has not there begun a career, at the end of which looms the guillotine or the pistol-snap of the suicide. All who fall on the pavement of Paris rebound against these yellow-gray walls, on which a philanthropist who was not a speculator might read a justification of the numerous suicides complained of by hypocritical writers who are incapable of taking a step to prevent them—for that justification is written in that ante-room, like a preface to the dramas of the Morgue, or to those enacted on the Place de la Greve.

At this moment Colonel Chabert was sitting among these men—men with coarse faces, clothed in the horrible livery of misery, and silent at intervals, or talking in a low tone, for three gendarmes on duty paced to and fro, their sabres clattering on the floor.

"Do you recognize me?" said Derville to the old man, standing in front of him.

"Yes, sir," said Chabert, rising.

"If you are an honest man," Derville went on in an undertone, "how could you remain in my debt?"

The old soldier blushed as a young girl might when accused by her mother of a clandestine love affair.

"What! Madame Ferraud has not paid you?" cried he in a loud voice.

"Paid me?" said Derville. "She wrote to me that you were a swindler."

The Colonel cast up his eyes in a sublime impulse of horror and imprecation, as if to call heaven to witness to this fresh subterfuge.

"Monsieur," said he, in a voice that was calm by sheer huskiness, "get the gendarmes to allow me to go into the lock-up, and I will sign an order which will certainly be honored."

At a word from Derville to the sergeant he was allowed to take his client into the room, where Hyacinthe wrote a few lines, and addressed them to the Comtesse Ferraud.

"Send her that," said the soldier, "and you will be paid your costs and the money you advanced. Believe me, monsieur, if I have not shown you the gratitude I owe you for your kind offices, it is not the less there," and he laid his hand on his heart. "Yes, it is there, deep and sincere. But what can the unfortunate do? They live, and that is all."

"What!" said Derville. "Did you not stipulate for an allowance?"

"Do not speak of it!" cried the old man. "You cannot conceive how deep my contempt is for the outside life to which most men cling. I was suddenly attacked by a sickness—disgust of humanity. When I think that Napoleon is at Saint-Helena, everything on earth is a matter of indifference to me. I can no longer be a soldier; that is my only real grief. After all," he added with a gesture of childish simplicity, "it is better to enjoy luxury of feeling than of dress. For my part, I fear nobody's contempt."

And the Colonel sat down on his bench again.

Derville went away. On returning to his office, he sent Godeschal, at that time his second clerk, to the Comtesse Ferraud, who, on reading the note, at once paid the sum due to Comte Chabert's lawyer.

In 1840, towards the end of June, Godeschal, now himself an attorney, went to Ris with Derville, to whom he had succeeded. When they reached the avenue leading from the highroad to Bicetre, they saw, under one of the elm-trees by the wayside, one of those old, broken, and hoary paupers who have earned the Marshal's staff among beggars by living on at Bicetre as poor women live on at la Salpetriere. This man, one of the two thousand poor creatures who are lodged in the infirmary for the aged, was seated on a corner-stone, and seemed to have concentrated all his intelligence on an operation well known to these pensioners, which consists in drying their snuffy pocket-handkerchiefs in the sun, perhaps to save washing them. This old man had an attractive countenance. He was dressed in a reddish cloth wrapper-coat which the work-house affords to its inmates, a sort of horrible livery.

"I say, Derville," said Godeschal to his traveling companion, "look at that old fellow. Isn't he like those grotesque carved figures we get from Germany? And it is alive, perhaps it is happy."

Derville looked at the poor man through his eyeglass, and with a little exclamation of surprise he said:

"That old man, my dear fellow, is a whole poem, or, as the romantics say, a drama.—Did you ever meet the Comtesse Ferraud?"

"Yes; she is a clever woman, and agreeable; but rather too pious," said Godeschal.

"That old Bicetre pauper is her lawful husband, Comte Chabert, the old Colonel. She has had him sent here, no doubt. And if he is in this workhouse instead of living in a mansion, it is solely because he reminded the pretty Countess that he had taken her, like a hackney cab, on the street. I can remember now the tiger's glare she shot at him at that moment."

This opening having excited Godeschal's curiosity, Derville related the story here told.

Two days later, on Monday morning, as they returned to Paris, the two friends looked again at Bicetre, and Derville proposed that they should call on Colonel Chabert. Halfway up the avenue they found the old man sitting on the trunk of a felled tree. With his stick in one hand, he was amusing himself with drawing lines in the sand. On looking at him narrowly, they perceived that he had been breakfasting elsewhere than at Bicetre.

"Good-morning, Colonel Chabert," said Derville.

"Not Chabert! not Chabert! My name is Hyacinthe," replied the veteran. "I am no longer a man, I am No. 164, Room 7," he added, looking at Derville with timid anxiety, the fear of an old man and a child.—"Are you going to visit the man condemned to death?" he asked after a moment's silence. "He is not married! He is very lucky!"

"Poor fellow!" said Godeschal. "Would you like something to buy snuff?"

With all the simplicity of a street Arab, the Colonel eagerly held out his hand to the two strangers, who each gave him a twenty-franc piece; he thanked them with a puzzled look, saying:

"Brave troopers!"

He ported arms, pretended to take aim at them, and shouted with a smile:

"Fire! both arms! *Vive Napoleon*!" And he drew a flourish in the air with his stick.

"The nature of his wound has no doubt made him childish," said Derville.

"Childish! he?" said another old pauper, who was looking on. "Why, there are days when you had better not tread on his corns. He is an old rogue, full of philosophy and imagination. But to-day, what can you expect! He has had his Monday treat.—He was here, monsieur, so long ago as 1820. At that time a Prussian officer, whose chaise was crawling up the hill of Villejuif, came by on foot. We two were together, Hyacinthe and I, by the roadside. The officer, as he walked, was talking to another, a Russian, or some animal of the same species, and when the Prussian saw the old boy, just to make fun, he said to him, 'Here is an old cavalry man who must have been at Rossbach.'—'I was too young to be there,' said Hyacinthe. 'But I was at Jena.' And the Prussian made off pretty quick, without asking any more questions."

"What a destiny!" exclaimed Derville. "Taken out of the Foundling Hospital to die in the Infirmary for the Aged, after helping Napoleon between whiles to conquer Egypt and Europe.— Do you know, my dear fellow," Derville went on after a pause, "there are in modern society three men who can never think well of the world—the priest, the doctor, and the man of law? And they wear black robes, perhaps because they are in mourning for every virtue and every illusion. The most hapless of the three is the lawyer. When a man comes in search of the priest, he is prompted by repentance, by remorse, by beliefs which make him interesting, which elevate him and comfort the soul of the intercessor whose task will bring him a sort of gladness; he purifies, repairs and reconciles. But we lawyers, we see the same evil feelings repeated again and again, nothing can correct them; our offices are sewers which can never be cleansed.

"How many things have I learned in the exercise of my profession! I have seen a father die in a garret, deserted by two daughters, to whom he had given forty thousand francs a year! I have known wills burned; I have seen mothers robbing their children, wives killing their husbands, and working on the love they could inspire to make the men idiotic or mad, that they might live in peace with a lover. I have seen women teaching the child of their marriage such tastes as must bring it to the grave in order to benefit the child of an illicit affection. I could not tell you all I have seen, for I have seen crimes against which justice is impotent. In short, all the horrors that romancers suppose they have invented are still below the truth. You will know something of these pretty things; as for me, I am going to live in the country with my wife. I have a horror of Paris."

"I have seen plenty of them already in Desroches' office," replied Godeschal.

PARIS, February-March 1832.

BOOKS PUBLISHED BY
PHAROS BOOKS

sales@pharosbooks.in   011 40395855   www.pharosbooks.in

Plot No.-63, 1st Floor, Main Mother Dairy Road, Pandav Nagar Delhi-110092